#Holiday

A Hashtag Holiday Short Story

(Hashtag Series #7)

Plus festive recipes to fill your tummy and warm your heart.

Givers Gonna Give…

Published by: Cambria Hebert Books, LLC

http://www.cambriahebert.com

Interior design and typesetting by Sharon Kay of Amber Leaf Publishing
Cover design by MAE I DESIGN
Edited by Cassie McCown of Gathering Leaves Editing
Copyright 2015 by Cambria Hebert

This is a work of fiction. Names, characters, places, and incidents either are the product of the author's imagination or are used fictitiously, and any resemblance to actual persons, living or dead, business establishments, events, or locales, is entirely coincidental.

Paperback ISBN: 978-1-946836-10-6

Twas the night of game day,

And all through the town,

Lacey, glittering snowflakes fluttered around.

They clung to the roads, concealing everything with white.

It was a beautiful #holiday sight.

The paparazzi were out without any care,

In hopes to catch Romeo and Rimmel, rumored to be there.

When out on the road there arose such a clatter.

The Hellcat spun out, but it shouldn't matter.

I pulled out my cell to dial in a flash.

But the battery was dead. What useless trash.

The moonlight glistening on the new fallen snow

Made us forget we needed a tow.

For the season was upon us. Our family was alight.

Our #holiday was destined to be merry and bright.

#Holiday

by Cambria Hebert

"Christmas isn't a season.
It's a feeling."
-Edna Ferber
#PutJoyInYourSpirit
#BuzzBoss

ROMEO

One wasn't supposed to be annoyed on Christmas Eve, but that's exactly what I was.

We'd just finished a brutal game, taking the win by the skin of our teeth. The winter wind had whipped around us on the field so hard there was more than one moment I gripped the ball and wondered why the fuck the game was even being played.

Some of the passes I'd thrown would have been perfect if not for that gusty, wicked wind. It damn near pulled the ball right into the other team's hands on more than one occasion.

So I wised up. I started throwing into the wind.

Why fight against something when you could just use it to your own advantage?

It had been a ballsy move, but fuck.

I hated feeling like I had to claw my way to a win. It wasn't that I minded the work, but it took a lot of energy, and I was tired.

Plus, it was Christmas Eve. As much as I loved football, I loved Rim more. Knowing I could be home beside a crackling fire, with white lights twinkling in the tree, the sounds of my family, and my wife in my lap...

It made the blustery weather that much more bitter.

The National Football League usually tried to stay away from holiday games. They realized it was a sort of hardship to ask us all to play when most everyone else was enjoying the season... but there was usually still a Christmas Eve game.

And the Knights just happened to be in it this year.

Our record this season was kickass. Despite the rocky nature of our team relationships when I took over the starting quarterback position, me, B, and the rest of the guys had plowed through it just like we did the end zone.

I'd always doubted the Knights would ever feel as much like home as the Wolves had, but those doubts were in the past.

If the rapport and loyalty I felt in the locker room hadn't been proof enough, the fact that we were literally on the fast track to the Super Bowl was.

We were going to make it to the big game. We were going to win. Especially after tonight.

When we did, me and my team would be that much closer.

The snow, frigid temperatures, and the date weren't even enough to stop us.

My body was sore, my shoulder ached, and I wanted a beer.

A blowjob might be nice, too...

But none of that was why I was so annoyed.

Nope.

I was annoyed because the paparazzi was stalking us.

You'd think since they had the choice to be home with their families, that would have won out over following around some guy they didn't even really know.

But that was the thing.

They weren't following me.

It was Rim they wanted a piece of.

Even before we got married, the press loved her. She was photographed at games, at any event she went to with me… Hell, they even photographed us out on the street for no reason at all. Her clothes, her hair, the ring I slid on her finger… It was all fair game.

And now they were constantly looking for something else.

What all the damn magazines so "affectionately" called the baby bump.

Seemed our marriage, my winning season, and the fact we were building a house with a gate was a clear indication that soon, she would have a little football player in her belly.

While I rather liked the idea, it wasn't exactly accurate.

The press didn't care about accuracy, though. They only wanted to sell their rags off grocery store shelves.

Rags = gossip magazines.

Rim with my baby growing inside her was quite the hot sell. It didn't matter that she wasn't pregnant, that we never even said we were *trying* to get pregnant.

The Knights quarterback baby watch was officially underway. All the hoodies and coats Rim wore were now just an excuse to hide her growing bump.

My wife being followed and stared at, constantly photographed, pissed me off.

What's worse?

It made her anxious. The attention wasn't welcome, and as good as she was about dealing with it all, I knew she was growing weary and fearful.

It's true my little niece, Nova, had been the reason we put the family compound on the fast track, but even if she hadn't come along, I'd still be hitting the gas on the house.

Rim needed somewhere safe and away from the prying eyes of the public.

Hell, at this point, we all did.

The reporters were like vultures standing outside the box where Rim and Ivy sat for the game. It was colder than a thirty-year-old virgin's vagina outside, so they couldn't sit in the stands.

B and I shared a look as we shouldered our way through and slipped through the door. I could tell by the way his dark eyes gleamed and the rigid set of his jaw that he was just as pissy and tired as I was tonight.

The press had been equally aggressive about getting pictures of Nova. And that meant Braeden was basically a walking time bomb.

No one could even look at that little girl with anything other than sheer adoration or he was ready to throw down right there.

And, yes… I admit…

I might have been the same way.

What? She was freaking adorable.

My eyes sought out Rimmel the second the door closed behind us. She was close by, standing beside Ivy and a couple of the other team wives. Ron Gamble was on the other side of the room with what looked like a glass of eggnog in his hand.

Rimmel's entire body rotated toward me before her eyes even found mine. I smiled, the familiar feel of possession licking through my body like a flame. I fucking loved the way she automatically responded to my presence, as if she were so attuned to me it was second nature.

A smile stole over her features, and some of the irritation I felt was calmed. Even though we stared at one another, our eyes holding a private conversation of their own, my feet didn't carry me toward her.

Instead, Braeden and I made a beeline for the large gray baby seat near Ivy's feet. The corner of a thick pink blanket trailed over the side and brushed against the floor.

We crouched at the same time. Braeden gently slid the carrier around and easily pushed up the small canopy pulled over the top. I tucked the blanket back up inside the seat, and we both stared down at the newest addition to our family.

Nova was only three months old, but she pretty much ruled our house. She was sleeping peacefully, her lids closed, hiding the beautiful blue eyes she'd inherited from her mother. There was a pink pacifier in her mouth, and it moved in a steady motion as she sucked at it even as she slept.

On her head was a purple hat with an orange bow on the front. Knight colors. The rest of her tiny body was buried under blankets.

Braeden reached out one finger and caressed her cheek.

"Don't wake her," Ivy said, her voice low. "I just got her to sleep."

Satisfied my niece was all good, I stood and reached for Rim. "Hey, baby."

"Hey," she murmured, wrapping her arms around my midsection. "Rough game."

I grunted. "You ready to go?"

"Definitely." She pulled back and smiled up at me.

I couldn't wait to be alone with her. Her hand felt small in mine when I wrapped my palm around hers. I turned, and my steps faltered.

B was standing close by with Ivy folded against his chest. I knew just by the wide stance of his legs, the way he was holding Ivy against him, and the hard look in his eyes that he wasn't down for any kind of fight with the press.

The dark-colored beanie low on his forehead and slashing over his eyes did nothing to belay the ass-kicking attitude he projected.

"Rim and I will go out first and distract them. Take the baby and get the hell out of here fast," I told him. The last thing I wanted to do was deal with the press— or make Rim deal—but it was better us than B.

"Thank you," Ivy mouthed as B released her.

"Thanks, man." His voice was gruff as he reached for the handle on the baby carrier.

"Anytime," I said. "See you at the house."

He straightened, and his eyes went to Rim, a look of regret passing behind his dark gaze as he frowned.

Rimmel pulled away from me to lean up and peck him on the cheek. "I'm fine. I'd rather the press take pics of me than Nova."

"I feel like I'm throwing you to the wolves." He turned toward her.

"I like animals." She teased.

A small smile played on his lips. "Fine. See you at the cabin."

Rim waved and did a damn good job of looking like she couldn't care less about the press. I tucked my arm over her shoulders and held her tightly into my side as the four of us headed to the door.

After I nodded and waved to Gamble, we walked out the door. The second we did, flashbulbs started going off and reporters called our names.

I plastered a charming smile to my face and tugged Rim farther into my side. We moved just slightly toward the crowd and turned so the reporters would all be facing us and away from the door.

They were shouting out questions, and I smiled wider. "I hear you all are waiting for a baby announcement." I teased. A bad taste coated my mouth. Sometimes playing up to the press was such a chore.

But it worked.

Just like I knew, everyone focused on us, giving B and Ivy the perfect opportunity to slip out the door and rush down the hall toward the elevator.

Soon as they were out of sight, I breathed a sigh of relief.

"C'mon." I leaned down to speak into Rimmel's ear.

I started forward, but the crowd closed in. Rimmel stumbled at my side, and without thought, I swung her up into my arms.

"What about the baby?" someone yelled.

I ignored them and hurried toward the elevator. One of the reporters tried to get into the car with us when it slid open. I gave them a subtle reminder they weren't welcome.

Fine. I wasn't subtle. I told them if they got into the elevator with us, I'd shove the camera up their ass and take a pic of their colon.

Did I mention I was in a pissy mood?

We'd barely made it into the parking lot when several of the reporters came rushing out of the stairwell and trailed behind us.

And so here I was.

Tearing out of the parking lot and onto the main road. Snow was piled up on either side of the white lines, and the freshly fallen flakes still coated the trees.

Some of the more persistent paparazzi got into cars and tailed us.

Didn't these people ever give it a rest?

"You kind of implied back there we had a baby announcement," Rimmel observed. Her slim fingers curled around the door handle as she talked.

I thought it was cute the way she braced herself for the driving I was about to do.

Sad thing was she was used to it. This wasn't the first time we'd been followed by overzealous, nosy gossipmongers.

I cursed. "I was trying to buy B and Ivy some time, but that was clearly the wrong thing to say."

"Might not have been the best choice," she said weakly as I took a turn quickly.

I muttered a dark curse. "I'm sorry, baby. I wasn't thinking straight, and now you're going to be even more sought after."

"You've had a long night. This isn't your fault." Her voice was sure.

The fact she let me off the hook so easily and accepted her fate made me even more disgusted. I glanced in the rearview mirror. We were still being tailed.

Hell if I was going to lead them to the cabin we were all staying at.

Fuck that.

We rented a place sort of off the beaten path for a reason.

I made a sharp and sudden left down a side street. The sound of blaring horns made me grimace, but I kept going. I shot down the street and then steered abruptly back out onto the main road and shot through a light that had just turned red.

I glanced at Rim to make sure she was hanging in. She was. My girl was a fucking champ. And then I looked in the rearview.

One car was still trailing us.

It was a little hatchback. The Cat could outrun it for sure, but I wasn't going to go all *Fast and Furious* out here on Christmas Eve on a main road.

I took the right up ahead like I would normally to get to the cabin and then shot forward. The car following us turned, and I cussed.

"Hang on, baby." I gritted my teeth and made a left, then a right, and another right.

I shot down the one-lane empty road I'd somehow found my way to and didn't slow down until I was sure we'd lost all the reporters.

I sighed raggedly and let up on the gas. "I'm fucking sorry, Rim."

Her eyes widened behind her glasses and the light from the dash glinted off the lenses. "Why would you be sorry?"

"They were already fucking insistent, and I pretty much just dangled a shiny golden nugget in front of them." I picked up her hand and brought it to my lips. "I don't want this for you."

Gently, she pulled her hand from mine and brushed her palm over my stubbled jaw. "This is nothing," she whispered, leaning across the seats toward me. "Nothing in terms of what I would endure to have a life with you."

I slowed the car even more and rolled my head in her direction. "You shouldn't have to *endure* anything."

"Forget them," she whispered. Her lips curved into a smile, and I was sorry I had to glance back at the road and miss it. "It's our first Christmas Eve as husband and wife. We're staying in a gorgeous log cabin, and there is snow on the ground. Take me home, husband. Take me to bed."

A growl rumbled in my chest. I liked it on a very primitive level when she called me husband.

Since this was a back road and we were alone, I jerked the wheel to make a sharp U-turn right there in the center of the street. Rim wanted me to take her to bed, and I damn well was happy to oblige.

Unfortunately, my stellar driving was no match for the patch of black ice so well disguised on the dark pavement.

I felt the back tires lose traction before we started to fishtail. I resisted the urge to pound on the brakes, realizing it would only make us slide worse.

I did grip the wheel and attempt to right us. It was a lost effort.

The Hellcat was an awesome machine, but it wasn't exactly prime for handling icy back roads, and we spun in a full circle.

Rimmel made a sound of distress, and I released the wheel entirely and used my arm nearest her as an extra seatbelt to pin her back against the leather.

"Romeo!" she squealed as the car skidded sideways off the road and went back end first right into an imposing snow bank.

#HolidayAdvice

When life sends a blizzard, build a snowman.
#UseACarrotForTheNose

#BuzzBoss

BRAEDEN

It was my daughter's first Christmas.

Sure, she wasn't going to remember it, but I always would.

This wasn't how I wanted to spend it. Sneaking through the stadium, tension coiled between my shoulder blades, anticipating a fight when someone turned up with a camera.

I didn't mind so much being photographed. Sure, it was annoying as hell, and Romeo handled it better than me, but it was part of the job.

But my daughter didn't sign up for this shit.

I wasn't going to have it. I wouldn't allow Ivy and Nova to be stalked by the bloodsuckers just so they could make a couple bucks.

I'd give up football before I let that happen.

I felt bad because Rome and Rim pretty much took one for the team tonight. Fuck, I knew Romeo was just as annoyed as me, but I let him do it anyway. Looking at Rim, I almost relented and told them to disappear first. But I didn't. That old familiar rage that lurked deep inside me was a little too close to the surface for my comfort. Ever since I saw Nova in Ivy's arms and then held her in mine, it wasn't hard to stir it up when I felt my family was being threatened.

My family stepped up to the plate tonight, and I'd have to make it up to them somehow.

As I secured the infant seat into the back of the new white Range Rover I'd bought Ivy the second my pro pay hit the account, I didn't feel bad. I'd rack up a world of debt to keep this little girl safe and away from prying eyes.

When I pulled back to shut the door, Ivy slipped in quickly, sticking her head down close to her, making sure the baby was totally all right. It didn't matter I'd just done it. Ivy had to see for herself. Turns out she had quite the mother lion in her.

I fucking loved it.

When she was satisfied, her blond head, covered in a thick red cable-knit hat, pulled back. I shut the door gently, so as not to startle a sleeping Nova.

"Hi," I murmured, grasping her waist right at the place I called B handles and tugging her toward me. Fat, white flakes of snow fell lazily from the inky black sky and swirled around us. The tip of her nose was pink from the cold, and her dark lashes framed her wide eyes.

"Hey." The throaty quality of her voice tightened my abs.

"All I could think about tonight was being alone with you guys." I cupped the back of her neck and used my thumb to turn up her jaw.

"Me too," she murmured and leaned up to kiss me.

Her full lips felt cold against mine, and I opened for her, covering her mouth totally, offering her warmth amongst the snow.

I twisted my tongue against hers and caught the distinct flavor of peppermint, and I smiled against her lips. "Someone's been eating candy canes again," I murmured.

"Maybe." She giggled.

I wrapped both arms around her and lunged forward, bending her back and drinking in the full taste of her, with a little twist of peppermint.

This was how Christmas tasted.

It tasted like my wife, the love of my life. Like crisp wintry air and the sharp, sweet aftertaste of a candy cane.

It might be a taste better than sprinkles.

And that was saying something.

Her hands slid up like they wanted to tangle in my hair but couldn't, so they changed direction and wrapped around my ears.

She held on to the sides of my head while I kissed the shit right out of her, and I felt her knees weaken and my arms had to take on more of her weight to keep her from falling.

The rumble of an engine made my arms turn stiff around her. I lifted my head and twisted around to see a car pull right up beside the Range Rover on the driver's side.

Shit! I knew better than this. To get caught up in the parking lot of the stadium. We were trying to get away from the press, not give them something to photograph.

"In the car, baby," I said quietly and deftly opened the passenger door and ushered Ivy inside. When I tried to pull back and shut the door, she caught my hand. I glanced down, noting how pale and small hers looked in mine.

"B?"

"Hmm?" I glanced up.

"Let's just go, okay?"

It was her way of telling me to keep it in check. I let out a breath and nodded.

I prepared myself for the unpleasant encounter as I walked around the car. The second I stepped to the driver's side, the door of the car that had pulled up beside us opened. I braced myself for a camera and a ton of questions.

But it wasn't a reporter.

It was two girls. They were both dressed in Knight gear, including matching hats with huge orange pompoms on the top.

"Ohmigosh," the girl rushed, all but falling out of the driver's seat. "You're him."

I relaxed instantly. They were fans. Just overeager fans who sat in the parking lot waiting, hoping to catch a glimpse of one of the players.

I didn't really feel like being charming, but a guy had to do what a guy had to do. It was my job. These girls sat out in the cold on a freaking holiday to watch the Knights play. They'd been here to support us, and I wouldn't do one damn thing to make them regret it.

"Depends on which him you're talking about," I drawled and stepped forward to help her pick herself up off the ground.

"You're *the* Braeden Walker."

I chuckled. "I'm pretty sure I don't have a *the* before my name."

She giggled, and it didn't escape my notice that she took a little too long getting her "balance" after I helped her up.

So it was going to be like that.

That being the other part of my job. The women. Before Ivy, I would have been all *hells yeah* and *YOLO*, but not now. Now when a woman tried to be a little too friendly, my hackles rose. There was no way in hell these two bitches didn't know I wasn't married.

They knew.

They didn't care.

That made them no-good, dirty scrubs in my book.

As if to punctuate my thoughts, the girl from the passenger side came rushing around next to her friend. Her eyes were bright and they roamed over my body.

Obvious much?

I ran my tongue over my teeth and then smiled a lopsided smile. "You ladies been out here a while?"

The driver nodded. "We really wanted to meet you."

"Me?" I asked.

The both nodded enthusiastically, and yeah, some of my annoyance with their scrub-ish behavior melted. They were fans.

"You and Romeo light up the field." The girl from the passenger seat sighed. Her hair was short, not quite shoulder length, and the brown ends flipped up and out beneath the hat.

The Knight hoodie she was wearing wasn't overly large like the ones I was used to seeing on Ivy and Rim. It fit like it was supposed to, and she paired it with painted-on jeans and a pair of boots with purple socks sticking out the top.

Her friend had long blond hair that hung over her shoulders from beneath her hat. Her eyes were brown, and she had on a lot of makeup. Ivy wore makeup, but it never looked like that.

"I'll be sure to tell Romeo you said so," I said to the girl who'd just spoken, and I winked. She giggled and shifted closer to me. I kept my feet planted where they were because backing up was just rude. "The Knights appreciate you ladies coming out to support the team. Means a lot to us all."

"But especially to you?" the driver said and leaned forward, placing a hand on my arm.

"Of course," I said, smooth. "Did you want me to sign something?" I asked, wanting to get on with it.

"Please!" the brown-haired girl said fast. She hurried to the backseat of the car and reached in, bringing out a football. She handed me a gold marker and held it out with the ball. "Could you sign it to my brother? His name is Max. He's twelve, and you're his favorite player on the team. He's going to pass out when he opens this tomorrow."

For the first time since they started talking, I didn't have to fake a smile. "You sat out here to get your kid brother a signed football for Christmas?"

Her cheeks turned even pinker than they already were. It wasn't from the cold. "I'm a Knights fan, too," she hedged. "But not like Max. He has a big poster of you by his bed."

Well, I'd be damned. That made me feel like a fucking hero.

"Sa-weet," I sang as I scrawled my name and number on the football. Then I wrote his name on it and a big smiley face.

"Oh my God," she said when I gave it back to her. "Thank you so much!"

I grinned.

"Merry Christmas!" she shot out and then leapt at me. She was like half my size, so I caught her easily enough and hugged her, but with much less zealousness.

Finally, I peeled her off me and set her away.

"Well, it was awesome meeting you."

"Wait," the driver said. "Can you sign something for me?"

I turned on my fake smile. "Of course."

The gold marker was back in my face, and I took it, using my teeth to uncap it. Both girls watched me like I was some kind of elusive attraction.

I gave them a grin around the cap, and they both sighed.

"Where's your paper?" I asked the driver.

"Don't have one," she said and stepped forward.

The next thing I knew, she was thrusting her chest at me. "Can you sign my hoodie?" She pointed to a spot. "Right here."

I threw back my head and laughed.

What?

Come on. I'm a freaking red-blooded man, and when a woman shoves her boobs in my face and asks me to sign them, it's kinda flattering.

"You sure?" I asked.

It wasn't the first time I'd been asked to sign a boob.

At least this one was clothed.

"Oh, I'm sure." She batted her eyes.

I chuckled and used my left hand to hold the fabric tight while I scrawled my illegible signature across the top of her breast. When I was done, I handed her the marker.

"I'm never washing this shirt." She sighed.

"Merry Christmas, ladies. Thanks again for supporting the Knights." I glanced at the one with the little brother. "Tell Max I said hi."

They watched me as I slipped into the Ranger Rover. I barely opened the door wide enough to get in and then fired up the engine.

I didn't wait to drive away. I did so quickly and deftly, around my admirers, and left them in my rearview.

When we were almost to the edge of the lot, I looked over at Ivy, sheepish. She'd been watching me since I'd gotten in the car.

"More admirers?" she mused.

I relaxed a little. She wasn't pissed. Every time women threw themselves at me in front of her, it made me nervous. It was one thing to know your husband had fans and admirers, but to see them up close and trying to get personal was something else.

So far, Ivy handled it okay, with only a few moments of icy stares at some of the bolder fans.

"They sat outside waiting for me," I said.

When she didn't say anything else, I turned and looked at her. She looked away quickly, turning her head to stare out the passenger window.

I still saw.

I saw a look I recognized. A look I'd seen once before.

Wistful, almost jealous, but… not quite.

It left me unsettled.

I didn't like seeing that look in those blue eyes. It meant I wasn't doing my job.

"Hey." I reached for her, and at the same time, Nova made a noise and started fussing.

Ivy jumped up and turned, "It's okay, sweetheart," she crooned and started climbing into the backseat.

"Careful now," I told her and slowed the car. I knew better than to tell her not to. It took me weeks just to get her to sit in the front seat instead of in the back with the baby. If I told her it wasn't safe for her to be climbing around, she'd probably just start sitting back there again.

And yeah, maybe I sometimes climbed back there when I wasn't driving, too.

"I think she's hungry," Ivy said and then started talking in soothing tones to our daughter. Seconds later, her fussing subsided and the light suckling sounds of her with the pacifier filled the car.

"We're almost there," I said. "I shouldn't have let them talk to me so long." If I hadn't, we might be at the cabin by now, and Nova wouldn't be fussy.

"It's your job." Her understanding voice traveled up between the seats. "I'll text Drew, have him get a bottle ready."

When I came to a red light, I glanced back over my shoulder. Blond hair cascaded over her shoulders, and the red reflection framed her downturned face in the dark.

She was staring down at Nova, a small smile pulling the corners of her lips.

She loved that little girl. Our little girl. My little girl.

"Baby," I said, low.

She looked up, her eyes seeking mine.

"You know how much I love you, right?"

"Times two." She agreed.

The light changed, and I pushed the car forward.

Words weren't enough. Not tonight. Not on Christmas Eve. Not after the look I saw haunt the depths of her eyes.

#HolidayHumor
Sex is like snow. You never know how many inches you're going to get or how long it will last.
#SexLikeSnow
#BuzzBoss

ROMEO

Anxiety slammed into me and I shot forward before the car even totally stopped moving.

The music on the stereo had seemed nice before, but now it seemed loud and disruptive. I hit the button to shut it off as I reached for Rimmel.

"Are you okay?" I stressed. "Are you hurt?"

Rimmel let out a shuddering breath and pushed the glasses up on her nose. "I'm fine. What about you?"

"Who the fuck cares about me?" I spat and gripped her shoulders, resisting the urge to shake her. "Look at me, are you okay?"

Her hands were warm when they covered the sides of my face. "I'm fine, Romeo. We just slid off the road. It's not like we were in a crash."

My fingers delved into her hair and started gently probing around for any kind of bumps or knots. She might have hit her head on the window when the car hit the snowbank.

She made a sound. My eyes narrowed, fingers stilled. I gazed at her, trying to figure out where she was hurt.

She rolled her eyes.

The woman freaking rolled her eyes at me.

"Did you hit your head?" Rimmel inquired.

I screwed up my face. "What? No."

"Then you should remember there is no way I could have been hurt because you practically threw your body in front of mine. I barely even jolted when the car hit the bank."

"You didn't think I'd just sit over here like some pansy ass, did you?"

She pressed a hand to her chest in mock horror. "You mean the driver actually stay in the driver's seat and *drive*?"

"Are you sassing me, woman?"

"Who, me?"

I muttered, *"Who, me?"* and then smiled. "The car was going off the road. Nothing I could do about it. But your safety… that I could control."

Rim sighed my name like only she could. "Oh, Romeo." Her small fingers unlatched her seat belt, and she climbed over the stick shift and straddled my lap. "You're okay?"

"Long as you are, then, yeah."

She pushed the glasses up onto her head, like a headband, and leaned forward to touch our lips together. Without the black-framed eyewear in the way, I pushed close, grabbing her and letting my large hands consume her head. We kissed fiercely for a long moment, ravaging each other like we'd been apart for months.

Still palming her head, I pulled back and stared into her unfocused brown eyes. She had such beautiful eyes. Everyone always went on about blue eyes and green eyes. Brown eyes were so underrated. So much depth there, so much warmth. Rim had flecks of gold in hers, and even in the dark car, I could make out the way they shone.

I leaned forward, my shoulders coming off the seat, and pressed soft, light kisses to her lids, allowing my lips to drift over the bridge of her nose to kiss the tip.

"The things you do to me, Smalls." I spoke on a whispered sigh.

"I love you."

Every time she said those three words, my heart skipped a beat. Her love was the greatest thing that ever happened to me.

"I love you, too, baby." I pulled back, realizing we were on the side of the road and the car was sitting sideways in a pile of snow. "You sure you're okay?"

"Promise." She made a crossing motion over her heart.

"Stay here. I'm gonna go see how bad the Cat looks." I helped her back into the passenger seat.

Helped her = putting a hand on her ass and giving it a squeeze.

Outside of the interior of the car, the winter wind slapped me in the face, and I gritted my teeth against it. I didn't mind the cold, but I'd had just about e-fucking-nough of it tonight. Between the game and now this, I was done.

I shoved my hands into the pockets of my coat and walked around the back of the car. The Hellcat spun and then slid sideways into the bank. The rear passenger side was right up against the packed snow, and it didn't appear there was any body damage, but there might be a dent in the side once I pulled it away from the pile.

The tires looked okay, and I hadn't hit anything else. I guess it was a blessing this happened on a back road where there was nothing or no one to hit.

The Hellcat was sitting at a slight angle, but that's because the road sat up a little higher than the bank I'd slid onto.

No worries, though. I'd have us back on the road and at the cabin in no time.

The passenger door popped open, and Rimmel stuck her head out. I saw her grimace when the cold wind hit her.

"Get back in the car!" I told her.

"How does it look?" she ignored me and asked.

I gave the back end one last once-over and nodded. "All good. Now get back inside."

She stuck her tongue out at me before retreating back into the heated interior, and I thought once more tonight about a blowjob.

For as tired and sore as I was after the game, I was horny as hell.

When I was back in the driver's seat, I grabbed the wheel and took the car out of neutral. "We'll be home in just a few."

She settled back into the seat, snuggling into the Knight hoodie she wore.

I gave it some gas, and the engine responded, but the car didn't move. Instead, the sound of spinning tires and the back end shifting a little against the snowbank was all that happened.

I grunted and gave it a little more gas.

The same thing happened, but this time when I let up, the car slid backward just a fraction.

"Romeo?" Rimmel asked, her voice a little wary.

"It's all ice back there. The entire side of the road is coated in it. The snow pile probably started melting a little today when the sun was out but then refroze because of the frigid temps."

"Are we stuck?" she asked.

I didn't reply right away. Instead, I gave it another try, pumping the gas and milking the engine. Besides spinning out and creating a lot of noise, the car didn't move.

I muttered a dark curse and flung myself out of the seat and stomped back around the car. My jaw locked when I saw all I'd done in my attempt at driving us out was dig us deeper into the ice.

I thought about pushing the car out of it and up onto the road. I probably could, but the sneakers I was wearing didn't afford me much traction, and I'd likely slip around trying to find my footing to put my weight into the push.

Not to mention I'd need Rim to drive as I pushed to give us some advantage to pulling up the slight bank we were wedged in.

I wasn't sure how I felt about a woman who wasn't the best driver on a sunny spring day and who was kind of shitty at driving a stick shift trying to haul ass out of some ice while I stood behind the car and pushed…

Yeah, that might not be the best idea.

And I wouldn't say it out loud, but my shoulder ached and I honestly didn't want to risk injuring myself this late in the season and so close to the Super Bowl.

Being an injured quarterback sucked donkey balls. I wasn't about to hit replay on that.

I got back in the car and blew on my chilled fingers. Rimmel was watching me, so I pulled them away from my mouth and turned toward her. "We're stuck, but it's not that bad. I'll call B, and he can come help me get us out."

"Want me to help?" she asked. Her glasses were back on her nose, and behind them her eyes were hopeful.

"This is man's work, baby."

She made a face like I knew she would. I laughed and pulled out my phone and called up the phone screen and hit B's number.

The call dropped before it even started ringing. I pulled the phone away from my ear and looked at it.

"No signal," I spat and dropped it in the cup holder. "Let me see your phone, baby."

Rimmel pulled hers out of the kangaroo pocket on the hoodie and gave me a sheepish look. "The battery died."

I made a sound. "Your battery died? How the hell is that even possible? You never use it enough."

"I forgot to charge it last night, and well… Nova looked so cute tonight, I took a lot of pictures…" Her voice trailed away like she felt guilty.

"You're allowed to use your phone," I mused. "It's okay."

Her teeth sank into her lower lip.

I grabbed her hand and kissed it. "No worries."

I snatched my phone up and opened the door again. "Maybe I'll get a better signal out here."

I strode out into the center of the empty rode and held up the cell like I was on some weird commercial where I was asking everyone if they could "hear me now."

Rimmel appeared at my side, and I frowned. "You should stay in the car. It's cold out here."

She responded by pulling up the hood on her sweatshirt and pointedly looking at the phone. "You get service?"

"No," I grumped but tried B again anyway.

The call dropped again.

"You'd think we were in Timbuktu," I muttered.

"Let's walk up the road some." She pointed in the direction we'd come. "Maybe the closer we get to civilization, the better the service will get."

"I'll g—" I started, then cut myself off. I wasn't going to leave her here alone on a dark street. No fucking way. "Yeah, okay. Let's go. Let me shut the car off."

Once it was off and locked up, the keys in my pocket, I returned to Rim's side and held out my hand.

"Feel like a moonlit walk in the snow, Mrs. Anderson?"

"Sounds perfect for Christmas Eve, Mr. Anderson."

Funny being stuck out here with no cell service didn't seem so annoying anymore.

We started walking down the center of the road. Not one car had come this way since we'd been here. Clearly, coming this way had been a good strategy for eluding the press.

"It's pretty," Rim murmured and turned her face up toward the sky where the snowflakes fluttered down.

"You ever catch a snowflake on your tongue?" I asked, watching her.

She looked like an angel out here tonight.

"No," she replied, not looking away from the sky.

I stopped walking. "What the hell do you mean no?"

She giggled and glanced at me. "Grew up in Florida, remember?"

"You're killing me, Smalls." I sighed. "B and I used to spend all kinds of time outside eating snowflakes and making snow cones with Kool-Aid."

"I bet you two were adorable," she mused.

"Of course we were." I agreed. "Open your mouth. Stick out your tongue," I instructed.

She glanced at me again.

I lifted my face and did it. "Ahhhh," I said when my tongue was hanging out.

She laughed and followed suit. We stood there in the center of the road, making sounds and moving around to catch the snow.

"I caught one!" she said enthusiastically and started bouncing around. "It's cold!"

"Well, duh," I retorted, amused by her antics.

Her bouncing around proved to be a hazard to her health, and her sneaker slid on the road. Her small frame pitched to the side, and I acted fast, catching her around the waist, effectively stopping her from busting her ass.

"I gotcha," I told her.

She gave me a brilliant smile and then bent backward over my arm and opened her mouth again. Her slight pink tongue sought out the snow, and she giggled when a white flake landed there and melted instantly.

I loved her.

So fucking much.

Her innocence was something I would always admire. And something I would always protect.

"You're right. Catching them is fun." Rimmel looked up at me.

I pulled her close and kissed her. "Now we just need to find some Kool-Aid so you can have a snow cone."

"I've never made a snowman either."

"What the fuck kind of childhood did you even have?" I gasped in horror.

She laughed, but I saw the shadow sliver behind the happiness. I hadn't been thinking. I shouldn't have said that.

Rim picked up on my regret instantly, and she straightened. "Don't feel bad. We're having fun. You can tease me."

"This a hard time of year for you, baby?"

This wasn't our first Christmas together, but in a lot of ways, it was. Last year, she'd flown back to Florida and we'd celebrated when she got home. This was the first year we would be together on the actual holiday. It was our first one as husband and wife.

I realized I didn't really know about her traditions. Her childhood holiday memories. I wanted too, though. I wanted to know it all.

"Not hard," she answered. "Bittersweet at times."

"How?" I asked, wrapping my arms a little tighter around her waist.

"Christmas was always my mom's favorite holiday. We always celebrated big, you know? Big tree, lots of decorations. Christmas music played in the house, presents under the tree. We made cookies the entire month of December. All different kinds. Kiss cookies, Rice Krispie treats, chocolate chip... But always on Christmas Eve, we made snickerdoodles. They were her favorite. They're mine, too. She liked marshmallow crème in her hot chocolate, not regular marshmallows."

"Now that sounds like some good shit," I said, and my stomach growled.

She laughed lightly. "After she died..."

My arms tightened around her. Of course I knew her mother was gone. I knew the hows and the whys. I'd brushed away her tears because of it more than once. But it didn't lessen the impact every time Rimmel said those words. It made me ache for her. I don't know how a person dealt with the death of someone so close to them. It seemed like everywhere she looked, there would always be a reminder.

I asked her once what it was like—to grieve for a loved one who was no longer here.

Hard.

That's what she'd said. She'd looked at me with those intensely soulful eyes and said, "Hard." Maybe she couldn't understand how she did it either. Though, later that night, she'd kind of retreated into her head and she'd told me a person just learns to live without the one they lost.

I prayed to God I never had to learn to live without the woman in my arms.

"We still celebrated the holiday, of course." She went on, oblivious to my internal thoughts. "But it wasn't like it had been. We didn't decorate as much or eat as much candy. The hot chocolate got regular marshmallows even though when I would see the cream at the store, it made me smile. It was too hard for him." She meant her father. "So we kind of celebrated in the least painful way possible."

God. It sounded miserable.

"I do still make snickerdoodles every Christmas Eve," she mused. Then her throat cleared. "Well, except for tonight of course."

I didn't like that. Not at all.

Oh, hells no.

"Why the hell not?" I demanded.

Her eyes shot up to mine, the memories of the past clearing in the depths. "Because we're here? You had a game and we're at the cabin…"

Again. *Oh, hells no.*

"Fuck that," I said and took her hand and towed her along beside me. Her legs weren't as long as mine, so she trailed behind me. When she slipped again, I stopped and crouched low.

"Up you go," I said.

"You're kidding," she intoned.

"Do I look like I'm kidding?"

"Romeo."

"Rimmel." I cautioned. "Do it."

She climbed on my back, and I hooked my arms beneath her legs and adjusted her into a piggyback ride.

"Your shoulder," she worried beside my ear as I started walking again.

I glanced sideways at her from the corner of my eye. "What about it?"

"I know it's bothering you."

"How'd you know that?" I asked curiously.

"I know you, Roman Anderson. I watch you. Even when you don't see me, I do. You've basically become my hobby."

I started to laugh.

"So I know when your shoulder is hurting and it's hurting right now. That game was tough, and the wind…"

"My shoulder's okay, baby. Nothing some ice and rest won't fix. It's just been a long night."

"Put me down," she demanded.

"No."

She tried to kick me. I caught her foot and gave it a gentle squeeze. "How quickly you resort to violence."

"You're stupid," she intoned grumpily. But then she totally negated the rudeness by kissing the side of my ear.

I couldn't help but chuckle as I palmed the phone again. I held it up as we both stared at the glowing screen.

"Oh!" she cried right in my ear. "You have one bar now!"

"I'll just use this other ear over here." I gestured to the one she didn't yell in. "To call 'cause I'm pretty sure I'm not deaf in this one."

She gasped. "I'm sorry!"

"You're too easy, baby," I murmured and dialed B.

The phone connected and rang and rang. When his voicemail came on, I swore and pulled the phone down to call him again.

"Maybe he's busy." Rimmel observed.

"He ain't too busy to come haul us out of a ditch." As the line started ringing again, I glanced off down the road. I could see the turnoff for another, busier road in the distance.

At least I knew if we couldn't get anyone to answer their phone, I'd be able to jog down there and flag someone down. Or hell, I'd just leave the Cat there 'til morning and call a cab. We had shit to do.

"Romeo?" Braeden said into my ear just as I was about to give up.

"Need you, B," I said without any greeting. My toes were fucking cold, and standing out here had been fun, but Rimmel was gonna freeze. "In my attempt to get away from the fucking press, I ran the Cat into a snowbank. I'm stuck." I told him where we were and asked him to bring Trent or Drew to help push me out.

"Be right there," he spoke quickly, and I could hear him already moving around.

I pocketed the phone with a slight smile on my face. It was good to have family. Family who would haul their ass out into the cold on a holiday to dig you out.

I was a lucky man.

"He'll be here soon," I told Rim and turned back toward the car. "Let's get you back in the heat."

Her arms wrapped around my neck a little tighter (but not so tight to strangle me) and her chin came down to rest on my shoulder. I heard her soft sigh right against my ear. "I kinda like being stuck in the snow with you."

"It's not half bad." I agreed.

"How long do you think until B gets here?"

I hit the remote start button on the key fob for my car to get the heat pumping again as I walked. "Not sure, why?"

Her lips brushed my ear when she whispered, "Ever have a Christmas Eve blow job?"

I groaned. "No."

"Well, since you showed me how to catch snowflakes with my tongue, I think its only fair I show you what one is like…"

She licked my ear.

I damn near came in my pants right there.

I flung open the car door and flipped the seat up so we could climb in the back.

"Oh, baby," I murmured, crawling in behind her and slamming the car door. "As horny as I am, this will be the fastest fucking suck of your life."

Her tongue wet her lips and she reached for the waistband on my sweats. "I'm sure I can make it last long enough to be unforgettable." Her small, capable hand delved beneath the fabric and wrapped around my already rock-hard cock.

I melted against the seat with a moan and let her have her way with me.

She kept to her word. Even though I didn't last very long, she somehow drew it out just enough to brand it in the back of my mind forever.

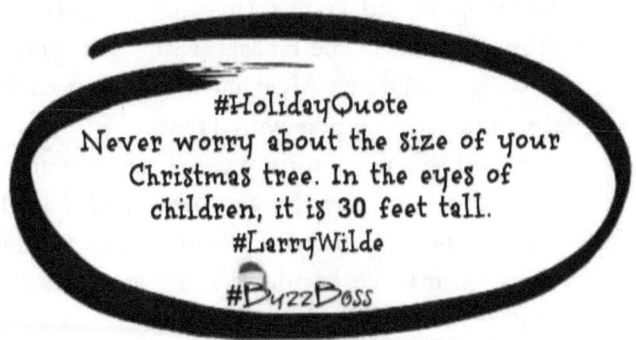

#HolidayQuote
Never worry about the size of your
Christmas tree. In the eyes of
children, it is 30 feet tall.
#LarryWilde

#BuzzBoss

BRAEDEN

Warm light spilled from the windows of the rented log cabin as we pulled up. It was a big place, with two stories, five bedrooms, five bathroom, and three fireplaces. The home was built of large, brown wooden logs all stacked up together to create the traditional cabin-style retreat.

Glass windows filled the walls, granting access to the view of the wooded lot the home was perched on. The driveway was a large gravel patch. Right now it was packed with snow and rock because trying to clear gravel the way one would pavement was a losing battle.

There was a two-car garage attached, but it was locked and tenants weren't given access. I figured the people who owned the place kept all their stuff in there for when they stayed. Probably was a lot easier than trying to haul all their shit back and forth every time they came.

I pulled up behind Trent's Mustang. It was covered in salt from the roads. The Hellcat wasn't here yet, but it would be soon. Drew's Mustang was parked back at our place, as he rode up here with Trent.

We rented this place for a week. Everyone arrived the day before yesterday. Since Rome and I had a Christmas Eve home game and a couple extra practices before New Year's, we decided to just work with the schedule instead of against it.

Renting a rustic cabin on snow-covered acres where our family could all chill for the holiday seemed like a pretty good idea anyway. Sure, our parents weren't too happy with us taking Nova out of town on her first Christmas, but since I had to be here, so did my girls, and we all made promises to celebrate just as soon as we got home.

Snow was still falling steadily. The irregular flakes stood out against the night as I shut off the engine and pocketed the keys.

Nova was fussing, and Ivy was trying to calm her when I climbed out and rushed around the back to open the door. By the time I made it, Ivy had the baby in her arms, cuddled against her chest, with one of the thick blankets covering her body and most of her head. She was still fussing, but it wasn't as prominent now because she was in her mother's arms.

I reached in, gently helping Ivy slide across the backseat, and practically lifted them both out of the car, placing her carefully beside me. Once I had the empty baby seat and all the other crap that came with having a baby (seriously, babies needed like a shit ton of stuff) clutched in my one arm, we headed toward the front door.

Without thought, my palm settled against the small of Ivy's back as we walked, and I kept an eye out for any patches of ice. The wooden front door was wide and had a huge pine wreath hanging in the center with a simple red bow. It swung inward, and Drew stepped out. In his hand was a bottle.

"What the hell took you so long to get here?" As he talked, his eyes swept over his sister and the baby as if he were making sure they were okay.

"The fans were waiting," Ivy said, stepping up onto the porch.

Drew grunted and stepped back for us to enter. "That place was a madhouse tonight."

"You guys got out okay?" I asked.

"We left a little early so we didn't get stuck in the traffic."

I nodded. I'd have done the same thing.

The door shut behind us, and Ivy shifted the baby so she was cradled in her arms and held her hand out for the bottle.

"Hells no." Drew denied and pulled the bottle away. "You aren't taking all the credit for this meal."

Ivy rolled her eyes as Drew reached for Nova.

Four men in this house. All four of us were freaking suckers for her.

She was squirming and fussing when he pulled her close, but the second he brought the bottle to her lips, the only sound to be heard was her gently sucking and grunting in pleasure.

Drew smiled down. "Who's the best uncle in the world?"

"Me," Trent said, walking into the entryway. "That was a beast of a game, man." He held his fist out for a pound. I obliged. "Props to you guys for pulling that shit off."

"Barely," I muttered.

The downstairs of the house was basically one great big room. There was a floor-to-ceiling stone fireplace centered on the far wall, and the fire was already crackling, the roasting wood creating a distinct scent. There was a gigantic sectional sofa near the fireplace, covered in pillows with a lot of bear, moose, and plaid on them.

The rug was thick over the older wood floors, and the walls were a neutral shade. The day we got here, the girls insisted on a tree and then picked out some huge eight-foot monstrosity I thought was ridiculous.

But whatevs, whatever made them happy.

I had to admit it had been pretty entertaining decorating the thing with tinsel, fake snow (more of that shit got on the floor than the tree) and a bunch of multicolored ornaments. My favorite decoration was the one that hung right in the center. It was a glass baby's first Christmas bulb with a big pink ribbon at the top.

Toward the back of the home was a huge kitchen with an island that could probably seat twenty people. The kitchen cabinets were cherry, and the granite counters were light. Even though the island was large enough for a small army, there was a large wooden dining table nearby that could seat eight.

All the décor in here was rustic and simple. Basically, it looked like a cabin to me. Hell, I didn't care as long as there was heat and the place was secure.

The girls seemed to like it, though. Ivy declared it had Christmas spirit, whatever the fuck that meant.

Drew carried the baby over to the couch and pulled the bottle out of her mouth to put her up on his shoulder. It never ceased to amaze me how easily we all learned how to take care of her.

She fussed, wanting the bottle back, and Drew gave her a lecture about not being a pig.

"Hey, man," I said. "You mind hanging with the critter a bit? I want some time with my girl."

Ivy made a sound at the use of the nickname I'd given Nova before she was even born. I admit one of the reasons I still called her that was because it drove her crazy.

"Are you kidding?" Drew said as Trent dropped down beside him on the couch. "I was hoping you two would leave."

"She needs a diaper change," Ivy said.

"That's what Trent's for," Drew quipped.

Trent rolled his eyes but nodded. "Go. We got this."

Ivy put the diaper bag I'd brought in from the car on the large stone-topped coffee table, and Trent winked at her. "Only for you, Ivy, would I change a diaper."

Ivy laughed, and I reminded myself that Trent wasn't flirting with her. He was just being her family.

I grabbed Ivy around the waist and towed her back toward the stairs.

"If you need anything…" she hedged, watching the baby.

"We won't," Drew said, not even looking up from Nova. Trent was already leaning over him to stare at the baby, too.

"C'mon, Blondie," I said gently. "She'll be fine. We're only going upstairs."

I felt her hesitation, but I pulled her along anyway. Time alone wasn't something we got very much these days, and the more I thought about it, the more I realized what a problem that was.

We were still newlyweds, and I fucking loved my daughter more than my own life, but I couldn't allow Ivy and me to become just parents. We had to be husband and wife, too.

Our bedroom was a big square room with a big king-size bed with a wooden frame. There were matching wooden nightstands on each side and a large patterned rug on the floor. Near the door leading into the bathroom was a stone fireplace, a smaller version of the one downstairs. I had the wood and kindling already laid out, so I took a few moments to get it lit.

When I turned back, Ivy had taken off her hoodie, hat, and boots, leaving the clothes in a heap on a nearby leather club chair. She was left in a pair of black leggings, knee-high purple socks, and a long-sleeve white T-shirt.

I pulled off my jacket and long-sleeved T-shirt and dropped it on the floor. After I kicked off my shoes and unbuttoned the top of my jeans, I prowled across the room.

I could feel Ivy's gaze. I knew she wanted me. I liked feeling her desire. I liked the way her eyes turned dark and just a little hungry. The way her tongue jetted out and wet her lower lip made me want to suck it into my mouth and never let go.

I stopped just shy of our bodies coming into contact. I bent, my lips hovering inches above hers, and held her blue gaze with mine.

I could take her right then. She'd open up for me. The longing and anticipation in her stare erupted a private war inside me.

Fuck, I wanted her.

I wanted her just as much as I had that first night on the beach. The night I practically attacked her with my desperation.

But I didn't just want her now.

I loved her, too.

There wasn't a single part of me that wasn't wholly hers. Ivy was everything. She was the past I'd always run from, the future I desperately wanted. She was my present, my heart, and the sight my eyes craved most.

It was because of that I didn't take her.

I would.

But first. First, I was going to get to the bottom of the feeling I got earlier in the car.

With no rush at all, I lowered my lips a fraction closer. Her eyes drifted shut and a small sigh parted her lips.

My heart skipped a beat. I held myself there for a few seconds, just reveling in the closeness.

Her eyes snapped open when I pulled back. Confusion made her forehead wrinkle. I took her hand with a light laugh.

"Come on."

"Where are we going?"

I led her the short distance into the bathroom where a huge claw-foot tub sat beside a large glass window overlooking the acreage. It was totally black out, but the falling snow looked sort of like a screensaver on a computer. The movement against the still backdrop was somehow soothing.

It also brought the outdoors in.

Ivy and I seemed to always be better in the outdoors.

I turned on the faucet and adjusted the handle until the tub was filling with very warm water. On the counter, there was a bottle of bubble bath Ivy had brought along but had yet to use. I snagged it up and dumped like half the bottle into the tub.

"That is way too much!" She gasped.

"Hush, woman," I told her and set it aside. The light scent of whatever the bubbles created swirled around. There weren't any candles in here, so I turned on the light in the water closet and pulled the door around and hit the switch for the bathroom.

The room plunged into shadows. The small amount of light filtering from the partially closed door was just enough to see, but not enough to disrupt the sight of the falling snow at the window.

"The baby," Ivy whispered.

"She's fine, sweetheart," I murmured and stepped up to her. "It's just you and me right now." I kissed her forehead and then her temple. Her hand splayed out across my bare side, and I made short work of my jeans and boxers, kicking the fabric away.

She lifted her arms when I tugged at her shirt and then deftly unclasped her bra. I murmured something I didn't hear when my eyes focused on her breasts.

They were perfect, slightly larger since she gave birth to Nova, and I'd learned more sensitive. Her nipples were tight, having puckered the instant I pulled away the bra. I filled my palms with their silky weight and squeezed gently.

Ivy moaned and her head fell back a little, her eyes closed. I rolled both nipples between my thumbs and fingers, gently pinching and pulling.

A shudder moved up her back, and I realized something.

"You're so hungry," I murmured, sinking a little low in my stance and hunching myself a little closer.

"What?" She lifted her head, her voice thick with desire.

"Ivy, baby, why didn't you tell me you were so hungry for me?"

She looked away.

Even though I wanted to demand an answer, even though impatience slammed through me, those feelings were eclipsed by the sensation of her flesh in my palms. I'd never hurt her. I'd never be rough with her out of frustration or even out of greedy desire.

I didn't acknowledge her silence. Instead, I continued to play with her breasts. The way her thighs pressed together and her hips rotated unperceptively told me how much she liked it.

I glanced over my shoulder, making sure the water level on the tub wasn't too high, and then turned back. I used my nose to nudge her chin up and then I trailed my lips down her neck with hot, wet kisses. My hands kept kneading her breasts, which felt heavy with desire. She pushed them into my hands for more, and I increased the pressure, causing her moan to fill the bathroom.

Holy shit.

She was fucking turning me on and she didn't even have her pants off yet.

I traveled across her shoulder, down her chest, and licked between the valley of her breasts. I knew she wanted me to linger there, to pull a nipple between my teeth, but I didn't. Not yet. I kept going, sliding down her body until I knelt before her.

When my hands hooked into the waistband of her leggings, she stilled. "Braeden…"

Was that apprehension I heard in her tone?

What the fuck was that about?

"Baby?" I asked.

"I…" Her answered faltered when I pressed my mouth against her core. I let my hot breath blow out against the cotton of her pants, and her thighs shifted, spreading a little apart.

I smiled and pulled the pants down, removing her socks and panties at the same time. When she was completely naked in front of me, my palms dragged up her calves and around to the back of her thighs.

I could stare at her all damn day and never get tired of looking at her curves.

"Braeden," she whispered and tried to tug me up.

I stood, palming her hips and staring down.

Ivy slipped around me and shut off the water to the tub. There were so many bubbles they took up half of the room and hung over the top like whipped cream on a mug of cocoa.

Ivy kept her gaze averted and climbed quickly into the tub. I stared at her bare ass until it disappeared beneath the bubbles. I watched her hand scoop at them, pulling them close to pile around her...

Almost like...

"Are you hiding from me?"

Her eyes widened a fraction and a look of being found out filled her features.

Memories of the last few times we'd made love flooded back. Us in bed with the blankets, us in the dark, catching an hour before Nova woke us up. Ivy wearing my T-shirt and me pulling up the hem.

She was totally hiding herself from me.

I wanted to know why.

"Ivy," I growled.

"I was cold," she rebutted.

"That never mattered before," I shot out. "Remember all those nights in the bed of my truck, you totally naked with the blankets shoved around our feet? Out there in the open... The cold never bothered you then."

She turned to stare out the window.

But I wasn't going to be put off. I was like a damn dog with a new bone.

"I know we haven't been able to have sex like we used to with your body having to recover from having the baby, then the nights we never got any sleep..."

Hell, I craved her almost every second of every day. I craved her the minute I left her body. I didn't push it, though. She'd just had a baby, for Christ's sakes. Between that and my football schedule, we were both exhausted.

I hadn't realized until a few moments ago that maybe she'd craved me just as much. Did she think I didn't want her anymore? Was the break I was trying to give her body being received as a rebuff?

I walked over to the side of the tub and crouched down so we were almost eye level. "Ivy, you know I still want you, don't you?"

Since her face was turned away, I watched her reflection in the glass. Her lower lip wobbled.

Aww, fuck.

"I'm sorry," she whispered.

"What're you sorry for?" I gripped the rounded edges of the tub.

"I'm fat," she burst out.

Wait. What?

It took me a minute for the statement to sink in. "You think you're fat?"

She turned toward me abruptly. "I don't look the way I did before I had Nova. I don't look like the girls who throw themselves at you all the time, like the ones in the parking lot tonight. I have stretch marks on my stomach. It's not as flat as it used to be, and my hips…"

I laughed.

I laughed so hard it had to be an ab workout.

I didn't stop until I got a face full of bubbles. "Hey!" I sputtered as warm water and white fuzzy soap clung to my face and chin. I wiped away the water from my eyes and blinked. "What the hell was that for?"

"Don't you laugh at me, Braeden James Walker."

"I can't help it, baby. You're being ridiculous."

Her lower lip wobbled again.

That wiped the humor out of me.

"Blondie," I said, serious.

"Sometimes I miss us," she said, so softly I had to strain to hear. "I love our little girl. I love her so much." She met my eyes so I could see she meant the words. But I knew. I knew how much she loved our daughter. "But there are times I don't like sharing you. I can't compete, Braeden."

"Compete with what, sweetheart?"

"With the young, sexy girls. With our baby daughter who has totally stolen your heart. Sometimes I worry I'm not enough."

Swiftly, I climbed into the tub and sank down into the overfull, warm water. It was so full some of it splashed over the sides and splattered onto the floor, but I ignored it. Ivy's knees were drawn up against her chest, and I spread my legs and slid her body in between them.

I tried to push down the sense of giddiness that overwhelmed my chest. It felt a sense of welcomed pressure over my heart, like a balloon that was about to burst.

I liked it.

But I didn't want Ivy to see that.

Clearly, she'd been torturing herself with these thoughts, and it hurt her. I wasn't about to let on that her possessiveness over me was something I fucking loved. Besides, she really had no reason to feel this way. She was it for me.

"What kind of mother feels jealous of her own daughter?" Her voice was hoarse.

"One who needs some lovin' from her husband," I drawled and hooked my hands beneath her elbows. The way I saw it, this was completely and totally my fault. She wouldn't feel left out if I was giving her everything she needed.

She glanced up, and I caught her eyes and held. Even though I didn't grip her chin, she didn't look away. My stare was like a net she'd gotten caught in.

"Why didn't you tell me you were feeling this way?"

"No guy wants to hear his baby mama drama."

I laughed. "Baby mama drama?"

"Sounds like something you'd say…" she muttered.

I couldn't stop the wide grin from splitting my face. "I fucking love you so goddamn much."

Her eyes snapped back to mine. "You better not cuss like that in front of our daughter."

"I only cuss like that for you, baby." I released her elbows and hooked my palms beneath her arms and lifted so she could straddle my waist. I leaned back against the porcelain of the tub and let my eyes roam her sudsy body.

I felt her shrink a little beneath my gaze, so I reached up and softly brushed away the bubbles, revealing all of her. "Your body has changed since Nova, but I like it more." I brushed a little more, deliberately skimming my knuckles over her already pebbled nipple.

I felt her listening even though she didn't say a word. She was weighing my words, the way my voice sounded when I said them. She was trying to decide if I was being honest or just telling her what she wanted to hear.

I weighed the fullness of her breast in my palm. "You fill my hands with softness when I touch you." I released her breast. My hand roamed down her side to her waist, where it dipped in, then gave way to the curve of her hip. "My hands never get bored when they explore your body, the peaks and valleys, the way your hips flare out and the roundness of your ass." As I spoke, my hand went to her middle, rubbing over the smooth skin. I felt her flinch slightly. I knew then this area was the place she was most insecure about.

No, it wasn't as flat and tight as it used to be, but I didn't care. In my eyes, Ivy was perfect, and nothing would ever change that.

"You carried my child in here," I whispered and pressed more firmly against her middle. "You accepted part of me into you, and you nourished it for nine long months. The stretch marks—hardly noticeable by the way—that cover this area are reminders of what you did for me. For us. Every time I see them, I'm reminded of the way you looked with a rounded belly and the way it felt to feel our daughter kicking just beneath your skin."

Her posture became less rigid. Her breathing became deeper, and her fingers found the sides of my waist and dug in.

She believed me.

I knew she would because I spoke nothing but the truth.

"I don't even notice the girls at the field, Blondie. I smile and wink because it's my job. But in the back of mind, I'm thinking about you. About getting you beneath me. About filling my mouth with your taste and filling your body with my cock."

"Really?"

I swiped my thumb along her lower lip. "You are the sexiest woman I have ever seen. There is no competition. You're my number one and you always will be."

"I've missed you," she said for the second time tonight.

"I'm so sorry, baby. I've missed you, too." I rotated my hips so my erect cock could nudge against her.

Because she was straddling my waist, my swollen head slid against her bottom, slipping between her cheeks just slightly.

I moaned because it felt good, the way my tip slipped in just right.

Her fingers tightened on my skin, and she rocked a little, pushing herself back into my cock a little more.

I gripped her hips at the sensations rippling through me.

I wasn't close to entering her. The way she was sitting made that impossible, but I was so hard. I wanted her so bad just sliding my sensitive cock between her cheeks made me shudder with pleasure.

"You like that," she murmured and lifted herself up just a little and slid back so my rod slipped all along her crack.

My head fell back and my hips jutted up. My dick was so hard it stood upward, and when she moved, the head brushed over her puckered, tight hole.

She sucked in a breath and stilled. But she didn't move away.

I cracked one eye and studied her. Her teeth were chewing her lower lip and her eyes were unfocused.

Interesting.

I moved again, repeating the same movement.

Ivy moaned.

This time, I delved my hand beneath the surface of the water and found her swollen clit. I rolled it between my thumb and finger at the same time I moved against her ass again.

I didn't enter. I didn't even try. I just let my head nudge the nerve endings in that spot.

Her legs started shaking and her eyes popped open to look at me.

"I…" I saw the wariness there.

I also saw the trust.

If I tried anything back there, if I made like I wanted to enter that part of her, she'd let me. She'd give me any part of herself I wanted.

"Not tonight, baby," I whispered and lifted her hips so I could position my cock at her slick, hot entrance. "But maybe someday. Something tells me you'd like it."

She made a sound and sank down on my length with one long movement.

Both of us groaned.

I held her hips, but she drove, rocking against me, keeping me so deep inside. The way it felt when her walls would brush up against that sensitive spot at my tip was the closest thing I'd ever get to heaven on earth.

As she moved, her breathing became labored. She squirmed on me, seeking out sweet release, but she wasn't finding it.

I sat up, wrapped my arms around her waist, and slipped my tongue into her mouth. At the same time, I drove upward with my hips, and she bore down. Our cores rocked together as I kissed her, and then she started to moan.

Her whole body came apart in my arms. She shuddered and quaked, and I kept moving, kept hitting the spot that drove her over the edge.

And then suddenly I was coming. My cock pumped into her. Every jerk it made ripped another sound from the back of my throat.

Ivy's hands fisted in the hair at the back of my neck. It was longer than it used to be. She told me once she liked grabbing onto it when we were making love, and I hadn't cut it since.

Her chest was rising and falling rapidly when I pulled back just enough to look into her unfocused eyes.

"I'm going to make more time for just us," I vowed, kissing her softly. "We have four other people that live with us, and my mother is right across town. We can be parents to our daughter, but we can also be Braeden and Ivy just like we used to be."

"I really want that," she whispered, and I felt her inner walls clench around me.

New stirrings of desire rolled over me like an avalanche.

"You feel okay?" I asked, hoarse. "That didn't hurt?"

"It was perfect. We can have sex as much as we used to, B. I'm totally healed."

Hells yeah. My cock started to grow hard again.

Ivy felt it, and the corners of her lips turned up. "Already?" She lifted a brow.

"You gave me the greenlight. You're never going to get any rest now, woman."

Her laugh was throaty, but she climbed off my lap.

"Where do you think you're going?"

"Not far." She settled between my legs and grabbed onto my shaft. The ends of her hair were wet and floated out around her in the water. She grabbed a nearby sponge thing she brought and added some soap. I submitted to her hands as she washed me thoroughly. Then I returned the favor.

The whole time I washed her, I whispered to her how beautiful she was to me and how much I loved her body. I really fucking did. I don't know where she ever got the idea she was fat, because she wasn't. But I didn't lecture her. I just drove her to near orgasm with my hands.

When she was whimpering my name and I was so hard it hurt, I got out of the tub, lifting her with me like she weighed nothing more than a single feather.

Since we were both soaking wet, I didn't lay her on the bed. Instead, I spread out a thick quilt on the floor right in front of the hearth and laid her completely naked body out before me as a feast for my eyes.

I made slow love to her right there beside the crackling Christmas Eve fire until we were both spent and weak limbed.

We were completely dry and totally drowsy a long time later when somewhere in the room my cell phone started ringing.

I didn't want to answer it, but it wouldn't stop ringing, so eventually, I found it in my discarded jeans.

"Rome?" I answered, wondering why he was calling and not just knocking on the bedroom door.

I wondered if we'd been loud and everyone knew what we were doing in here.

I decided I didn't care.

"Need you, B," he replied.

I listened intently as he spoke quickly.

"Be right there," I said and reached for some clothes.

#HolidayTruth
Men can do their Christmas shopping
for 25 relatives in 25 minutes on
Christmas Eve.
#ProcrastinatorsUnite

#BuzzBoss

ROMEO

My pants were fully in place. We'd moved from the backseat to the front by the time B pulled up in the white Range Rover Evoque he'd bought for Ivy before she had Nova.

I was still in a state of bliss.

Damn, my girl knew how to keep me happy.

Since she was cuddled up in my lap with her head on my shoulder and drifting off to the sound of the holiday music I'd found on a local radio station (hey, it's her tradition, and now that I knew about it, it was going to be *our* tradition), I didn't want to get up and wave them down.

I settled for rolling the window down and flinging my arm out as they rolled to a stop in the center of the road nearby.

The heavily tinted window of the Rover rolled down to reveal Braeden grinning like a smartass beneath the black beanie he was wearing. "Don't get up or anything," he called.

I gave him the finger. "Took you long enough!"

"I gotta say, Rome. I'm disappointed. I thought you were a better driver."

Trent's laughter floated out Braeden's window.

"Fucking garbage collectors were on my ass," I spat.

Braeden's face hardened, and he got out of the car, leaving it running. "Come on. Let's get you out of there. I left Ivy and the baby at the cabin with Drew."

"Baby," I murmured, and Rim stirred. "Over to your seat," I said gently and reluctantly lifted her off my lap to place her in the passenger seat. "B's here. I'm gonna help him."

"I'll help, too," she said, her eyes popping open.

"No way. Stay here."

She gave me a hard stare, and I gave it right back. I wasn't relenting on this. She could stay in the heat where I wouldn't have to worry about her turning into a Popsicle or falling on the ice and hurting herself.

"Fine," she muttered, sensing the hard stance I was taking.

I kissed her forehead and got out. B and Trent were standing at the back of the Rover, so I joined them. B lifted the floorboard of the trunk to reveal a place where he'd stashed half a hardware store.

"Damn, you rob Auto Zone?" Trent whistled.

"If there's ever a zombie apocalypse, I'm riding with you." I slapped B on the back.

He held up both his middle fingers, one for me and one for Trent.

"I ain't letting my wife and daughter go driving around without the shit they need."

"Does she even know how to use a carjack?" Trent asked, doubtful. "Or a flare gun?"

I snickered.

B slammed a bag of sand in Trent's middle, and he wheezed out a breath, then laughed.

"Is that some dried astronaut food?" I guffawed and pointed to some kind of long-term food supply. "Got any dehydrated ice cream?"

"I'm not the one stuck in the snow," B muttered and shut the lid.

"Aww, don't be mad, B." I followed him across the street to the back of the Cat.

He leaned in the window and waved at Rim. He popped open the door. "I came only for you, sis."

"BBFL!" she hollered.

I rolled my eyes.

Trent ripped open the sand and started dumping it behind the back tires and around them to give them some traction. When that was done, he added some around the front tires just for good measure.

"You drive out. Trent and I will push," Braeden said.

"You sure?" I questioned.

"Just don't run us down, huh?" Trent cracked.

B thought that was hilarious and he laughed hard.

I picked up a chunk of ice coated in snow and threw it at him. It bounced off his shoulder. Some of the powder exploded and hit him in the jaw.

"You did not just do that," B deadpanned.

"I'm thinking he did," Trent answered.

He made the same battle cry sound he'd been making since we were kids and scooped up his own huge pile of snow and hurled it at me.

Just like that, we were ten years old again.

Snowballs and insults went flying. Trent joined in and managed to get a good shot right in the back of my head. Snow coated my hair, and my fingers were red and numb, but I didn't care. We just kept on throwing snow.

"What on earth are you doing out here!" Rimmel yelled and popped out of the car.

Braeden launched a snowball at her. It hit the roof of the car and exploded.

She screeched and ducked. The next thing I knew, she was at my side, giving as good as she got.

The four of us played around longer than we should have, tackling each other and throwing snow. Both our cars still ran, and at one point I managed to face plant B right into a pile of white stuff.

It was a good time.

Finally, I called a truce when I noticed the way Rimmel flexed her fingers between throws in an attempt to give them some warmth.

After that, it didn't take us long to get the Hellcat back on the road. The first couple attempts resulted in some slipping, but ultimately, the sand and the muscle of two football players got us out.

On our way to the cabin, I made another unexpected turn. This one wasn't onto a back road, though.

It was into the parking lot of Walmart.

"What are we doing here?" Rimmel asked. Her nose was still pink from the cold.

"You need to get stuff to make those cookies," I said, sliding into a parking spot.

"It's already late," she hedged.

"It's still Christmas Eve." I pointed out. "A tradition's a tradition. Besides, I want to taste these cookies. I'm hungry."

She smiled, and I met her at the back of the car on the pavement. When she looked up at me, I took her face in my hands. "Just because we're together doesn't mean we can't still do the things you always loved to do. No more not doing something because we're too busy or because it might upset someone else. We're gonna make our own holiday, Rim. Your mom might not be here, but she's always going to be part of it."

"If you make me cry right now, my tears will freeze on my face."

I laughed. "No tears. Just cookies."

"Just cookies." She agreed, and we went inside the huge store.

About an hour later, we pulled up to the cabin, and I parked right behind the Rover. We managed to carry everything we'd bought inside in one trip and dumped it all on the giant island in the kitchen.

"What the hell, man?" B called out. "I thought you were stuck again. I was about to come out looking."

He and Ivy were sitting on the couch, the fire was going, and she was leaning right up against his chest, his arm folded around her and the baby in her arms.

Trent and Drew were also on the couch, and some Christmas movie was playing on the nearby TV.

"We had to make a stop." I tossed my coat nearby and stretched. "Rim's gonna make cookies."

"Good, I already ate like half the ones we had in there."

"I ate the other half," Trent said.

"Pigs," Ivy told them.

Drew laughed. "Seriously, though. I went to get some earlier and there weren't any."

"I'll make extra." Rimmel laughed and walked out of the kitchen carrying a large pack of ice in a towel. She reached out and set it on my shoulder in just the right spot.

"Thank, baby," I murmured.

"Hot tub out back," B said, glancing at my ice. "Might help with that."

I nodded thoughtfully. "Good call."

"Just don't freeze your balls off getting out to it," Drew quipped.

"Wanna go?" Rim asked.

I shook my head. "Cookies first."

"C'mon, then," Rim said. "I'll make you some cocoa. You can watch."

"I'm not watching." I grabbed her up and one arm carried her back into the kitchen. "I'm helping."

The entire time we made her mom's favorite cookies, she talked animatedly about the things she and her mom used to do around the holiday, and I listened aptly. Hell, it really didn't matter what she talked about. Just the sound of her voice drew me.

Even so, the stories were entertaining. Rim as a child had been even clumsier than she was now. Her voice and wistful tone (and I suspect the scent of baking cookies) drew everyone to the island, and before I knew it, there was a platter of warm snickerdoodles in front of us, cocoa heaped with marshmallow cream (it was better than regular marshmallows), and candy canes for stirring.

We all laughed and talked. It was the kind of time I'd hoped for when we rented this place. Not just because it was fun, but because this was family. It was what I wanted for Rim, for my niece, and even for myself.

There were a lot of things in life—good things, great things.

But this was the *best* thing.

We talked so long Rim had time to make up another pan of holiday Rice Krispie treats, and Ivy got in on the action and started making a pan of brownies.

B was getting out a huge container of red and green sprinkles when Nova started fussing in the nearby sleeper.

"I got her," I announced and went to pick her up. She wasn't wearing her hat anymore, and dark hair covered her head. It was the same color as B's. Dark hair and blue eyes.

This girl was likely going to give all of us gray hair.

She was crying when I tucked her into my arms. It was kind of like holding a football. Except she was more wiggly.

"Hey now," I murmured. "Ladies don't cry when Romeo holds 'em."

"What ladies would that be?" Rimmel asked from the other side of the room.

I made a face at the baby, and her eyes turned watchful. "Uh-oh. Don't be telling Auntie Rim about all the stories I've told you."

Without thought, I started swaying a little with her in my arms. Funny how three months ago, a baby seemed like an alien to me, and now holding one seemed as natural as breathing.

"Give the kid a cookie," Drew said.

Ivy laughed. "She needs teeth for that."

"Details," he muttered and then shoved another entire cookie in his mouth.

"She needs a bottle," Braeden said, coming toward me with a warm one in his hand.

I glanced down at her. She was still staring up at me, and my heart turned over. "I got it," I told him and snatched the bottle out of his hand. "Get outta here," I said. "I need some alone time with my niece."

Braeden obliged, joining Ivy at the island and making a big show of kissing her loudly.

I sat on the couch and propped my arm up to make the baby more comfortable. When the bottle was finished, she fell asleep on my shoulder, and the feel of her warm, small body made me drowsy.

The next thing I knew, the couch dipped, and I cracked open an eye, rubbing my hand over Nova's back.

Rimmel was looking at me with an odd expression.

"What?" I asked quietly, concerned but not wanting to wake the baby.

I could hear the family talking in the kitchen, and the scent of cookies and brownies swirled around in the air.

"Seeing you like that…" She began and smiled. "It's like a little glimpse in the future of what you're going to be like with our baby."

I reached for her hand to entwine our fingers. "I love him already."

Her eyes turned misty. "I know you do."

"You just say the word, Smalls. The second you're ready for one of these, we'll make it happen." I didn't want to push her. She was just finishing up school and finding her groove at the shelter she ran. We were busy and we were still newlyweds. But it would be a lie to say I didn't think about her with my child in her belly.

Rimmel smiled and gently fingered the soft hair on the baby's head. "She's beautiful."

"It's a damn shame," I said, forlorn.

Rimmel laughed low. "Even if she had four heads, you'd still say that."

I grinned fast. "Probably."

"Cookies are done," she said. "Thank you for helping me make them."

"Thanks for letting me eat them." I wagged my eyebrows.

"How's your shoulder?" she asked.

It was fine. The ice helped, and I hadn't thought about it in a while. But I didn't say that. "Could probably use a soak in the hot tub. You game?"

She nodded. "I'll go change."

She disappeared, and I carefully got up off the couch, supporting Nova's body. Trent appeared and settled himself into the cushions nearby.

"Baby duty," I announced and gestured to him.

He held out his arms, and I handed her over. Nova barely opened her eyes as he settled her against his chest.

A few seconds later, Drew sat near Trent, staring at the way he was holding the baby. It made me glance down to be sure she was comfortable before turning away completely.

She was fine, and so was Trent.

I had a feeling I knew what Drew's look was about, but I wasn't saying shit.

In the kitchen, Ivy was sitting on the counter and B was standing between her knees, holding her face as he kissed her.

I grunted. "Getting in the hot tub with Rim. Baby's with Trent."

B gave me a thumbs-up but didn't lift his mouth off Ivy's.

When Rim and I stepped out onto the expansive back deck, I wondered if maybe I was fucking insane to be out here to get in the hot tub. Snow fell harder than it did earlier, and our breath came out in great white clouds in front of our faces.

Rim was wearing my Alpha U hoodie over her bathing suit and clutched a towel. I swung her up into my arms and rushed toward the entertainment area of the deck.

In the center was a sunken-in round hot tub. The water was already bubbling and lit up because I'd come out here earlier to turn it on.

Nearby was a stone fire pit that ran on gas. One switch and it roared to life. That was going as well. A few lamps made to look like lanterns illuminated the space and the wintry air was tinted with the scent of chlorine from the water.

I stood Rim near the edge of the tub and shucked the shirt I was wearing. I'd forgotten my swim trunks, so I was just dressed in a pair of dark boxer briefs.

Rimmel watched as I stepped into the warm, bubbling water. It wasn't overly hot like some tubs. I'd been in a few that were almost unbearable, but this one was perfect. The heat on my legs was a direct contrast to the cold on my upper body. Snow gathered in my hair, and I rubbed my palm over the messy strands, feeling the snow soak in and make it damp.

I held out a hand to my wife, and she pulled her eyes off my body so she could remove the hoodie.

My mouth ran dry.

"Holy shit," I said, my hand falling down to my side.

She was wearing a red bikini. It left very little to the imagination. Fuck, her panties were bigger than the strings on this thing.

I was hard instantly.

I got hard so fast the world around me spun from the lack of blood to my brain.

I plunked down in the water, my ass hitting one of the bucket seats. I barely noticed how good the jets felt because my attention was totally on her hardened nipples, which were fully visible through the fabric.

"You like?" she asked, shy.

I laughed.

She shivered a little, and I stood abruptly and picked her up. Her legs wound around my waist and her front plastered against my chest. I wrapped my arms around her tightly at the same time my tongue delved between her lips, seeking out hers.

She groaned and opened, and I kissed her with more heat than this hot tub could ever generate. As we kissed, she rubbed her chest against mine and moaned every time her nipples hit me just right.

Snow swirled around us, melting the second it touched our skin. The bitter winter wind threatened our passion, but the steam from the hot tub rose up and created a veil around our bodies.

I sank slowly, taking her with me until I was back in the bucket seat and she was in my lap. Eagerly, I reached for the red string at the base of her neck and tugged. She gasped and pulled her mouth free.

"We aren't alone!"

"Yes, we are," I murmured and sucked at her collarbone. She moaned and arched into me. "I told them all to stay the hell in the house. And they can't see the hot tub from the windows."

"They know what we're doing out here," she whispered like it was some big secret.

"Baby, they know we have sex." I chuckled.

"But not when."

I answered her rebuttal with another kiss. A deep one. The kind that made her body boneless, and I felt her surrender. Moving deliberately, I reached up and dragged the red top off her chest. The second it hit the water, I let go and it was carried away by the current.

"You knew exactly what my reaction would be when you put that damn bikini on," I growled and bent my head toward her perky breast.

She whimpered when I latched on and suckled it into my mouth.

"Merry Christmas," she said between pants and rolled her hips into me as I worked her breast.

Best gift ever. Rim in a tiny bikini had been on my bucket list, and now… now it was crossed off.

I slid my hands up her back and palmed her shoulder blades, motioning for her to arch back, to offer herself up to me. She did, and I damn near shot a load in my boxers. Her creamy skin was completely exposed with two perfect mounds in the center with pink, tight buds just begging for attention.

Steam rose and snow fell. I scraped my teeth over her midsection and then dove into her breasts once more. I sucked and kissed every last inch of her chest. I did it so well she moaned my name and begged me with the movement of her hips. She ground against me so insistently I almost lost control.

But I wasn't done with her yet.

No way in hell. I set her away, in the seat directly across from me. Her eyes were unfocused and hazy. The confused sound she made felt like an award.

"Not yet, baby," I murmured and shoved my hand in the center of her legs. She shuddered, and I smiled. The silky wetness her body produced just for me was so prominent it mixed with the water in the hot tub.

I pulled back, and she watched me with hooded eyes (her glasses were in the house). The ends of her hair floated out around her, almost concealing her from sight.

I took it as a short reprieve and tried to bring the pounding of my desire down to a dull roar. I floated back to my seat and held her eyes, and I reached beneath the water and stripped off my boxers. The dark fabric floated to the top when I released them.

She bit her lip.

"You make me so effing hard," I whispered and took my throbbing cock in my fist.

She stared at the water, right where I was jacking myself, with rapt attention.

"I've never wanted anyone more in my entire life," I said rough as I ran my fingers over the tip of my head.

She pushed out of her seat and came toward me. I released my cock and arched forward so she could grab it instead.

She jacked me slowly, up and down, paying extra attention to the swollen head every time she drew near.

My hand went between her legs, and she opened for me. She was still beyond wet, and it made me happy. I thought by now the water of the hot tub would have washed it all away.

"We might need to get out in a few, baby," I said, hoarse, as she continued to work my rod. "Sex in a hot tub might not be too comfortable for you."

"I wanna try," she murmured as her fingers trailed down to my ball sack and squeezed lightly.

My head fell back, and I pushed two fingers inside her.

She played with my balls, and I played with her entrance until I was literally gritting my teeth to not come.

"No more, Rimmel." I pulled my hand away and gently pulled hers away as well. "I can't take anymore."

She reached beneath the water and untied one of the red strings. The fabric of the bikini bottom floated to the surface, and it was all the invitation I needed.

I gripped her hips and pulled her close. Her legs anchored around my waist, holding her there, and I surged upward in one great movement.

I penetrated her instantly. She cried out but then buried her face in my neck, likely afraid she'd been too loud.

I held myself still as a groan rumbled deep in my chest.

"I'm not going to be able to last," I said for the second time that night.

I couldn't help it. She was way too fucking hot. I was going to have to take a cold ass shower in the morning, then take my time making love to her by the fire in our room tomorrow night.

"Me either," she gasped and rocked against me.

I felt her body start to shudder lightly.

"You okay?" I asked, just needing to be sure. "In the water, it's okay?"

Her answer was a more thorough rock of her hips. My fingers dug into her thighs when I spread her legs a little wider, thrust up, and then gripped her ass. She came apart right there. I didn't even need to move. My cock was pulsating inside her so much it did all the work for us both.

Her teeth sank into my shoulder, and I clutched at her as an orgasm pulled us both under. When it released me from its sweet clutches, I was still hard, so I began to move. She met my movements with her own, and we rocked in blissful rhythm.

My cock was beginning to soften when she started to tighten up in my lap once more. Swiftly, I pushed my hand between our bodies and rubbed at her swollen bud.

Another climax took over her body, and I moaned along with her. She was fucking amazing.

She collapsed against me with a shudder, and I held her, keeping my cock tucked up inside her body for a long time.

I stared out at the falling snow, watched the crackling flames, and whispered to Rimmel how much I loved her.

When the heat of the tub started to grow uncomfortable, I pulled her back, and she made a sound of protest.

"Time to get out," I told her. "Too much heat. I'll hold you in bed."

Once I managed to put my wet boxers back on and wrap my waist in a towel, I held out a towel and motioned for her. She stood with the bikini clutched in her hands, and I wrapped it around her naked body and lifted her in my arms.

I carried her with me as I shut off the fire pit, hot tub, and outside lanterns. Once we gathered up our clothes, I made a dash for the house.

"You think everyone's still up?" she worried, looking down at her towel-covered form.

"Don't know." I stepped in the door off the kitchen.

Everything down here was quiet and no other voices could be heard. The only light in the whole downstairs was that of the Christmas tree.

"Looks like they're all in bed."

Rimmel gestured toward the clock on the microwave. "It's Christmas."

"Best Christmas I ever had," I said without doubt.

"Already?" she asked as I walked toward the stairs.

I stopped beside the glowing tree and kissed her gently. "Absolutely."

"Mine, too," she whispered.

#HolidayWish
All I want for Christmas is for the person reading this to be happy, healthy and filled with inner joy.
#HappyHoliday
#BuzzBoss

BRAEDEN

Nova was spoiled.

At three months old, she'd barely been in the world, and most of that time was spent sleeping and eating.

Frankly, I admired that about her.

All she had to do was breathe, and every person in the room was wrapped around her tiny little finger. Even though she had no clue it was Christmas Day and didn't know what a present was, she had more of them under the tree than anyone else.

Hell, than all of the rest of us combined.

She was the first one up, of course. I'd heard her fussing in the bassinet right beside the bed and jumped up to get her before Ivy was awakened.

"Shh," I told her softly, lifting her and cradling her against my chest. I grabbed up an extra blanket and tucked it around her before strolling toward the window on the other side of the room.

She looked up at me with wide blue eyes that were so much like Ivy's I was amazed.

"Mommy doesn't have to compete with you," I told her. "Because Mommy is the one who made you. It's like I said a long time ago, before you were even a thought. She's number one's mom."

Nova smiled.

There was nothing like it. I was the first person she smiled at.

It was because she liked me best.

When I announced that, there was voiced doubt she even smiled. Gas they said. A fluke. She was too little to smile…

Blah, blah, blah.

"Who loves her daddy?" I asked.

She smiled again.

See? She was totally smitten by me.

Her lower lip began to wobble, and I made a sound of distress. "Don't be starting that," I told her. "You know I can't handle it. You're all good. We're chilling."

I reached over and tugged the curtain back. The sun was up, which I thought was a bonus, and it had snowed all throughout the night. A fresh coat of thick white covered everything, making as far as I could see look like an untouched painting.

I tucked her a little closer into my chest, and she turned her head toward me, seeking a bottle. She was hungry, but I wasn't done holding her yet. Gently, I rocked her back and forth while I stared out at the snow and detailed all the things we would do when she was old enough to go out in it.

She was only a few months old and already I couldn't imagine my life without her. I couldn't imagine not loving her.

Sometimes it was a bittersweet feeling.

It made me reflect on what I didn't have with my own father. It made me wonder why he never felt this way about me.

I could only conclude that something was broken inside him.

It didn't matter, though, not anymore. He had passed. He'd never know the sweet girl in my arms, and though it was harsh, I counted it as a blessing.

I'd love this little girl enough for both of us, and she'd never know what it was like to have a father who didn't care.

She started fussing at me again, louder this time.

"Shh," I murmured. "Mommy's sleeping. We don't need none of her baby momma drama up in here on Christmas."

"I knew it was something you'd say." Her drowsy voice came from behind.

I glanced over my shoulder and smiled. "You weren't supposed to hear that."

Her laugh was throaty, and it reminded me of the sounds she made late last night when I woke her with my mouth between her thighs.

She pushed herself up to lean against the headboard and held out her hand.

Me and Nova climbed on the bed and settled beside her. Ivy cooed at the baby and laid her head on my shoulder. I kissed the top of her head and reveled in the moment.

Yeah, I guess I still had darkness in me.

But there was light now, too.

So much light.

Nova started crying, and Ivy leaned sideways to grab her pacifier off the nightstand and slip it into her eager mouth.

"I'll go make her a bottle," she said and started to slide away.

"Not so fast," I growled and towed her back with my free arm. When she was against my side, I tilted up her chin and covered her mouth with mine. Before fully pulling away, I pressed one last soft kiss to the center of her slightly swollen lips. "Merry Christmas, baby," I murmured. "I love you."

"I love you, too, B."

Nova made a noise, and we grinned at each other and got out of bed. I waited for Ivy to put on a pair leggings, furry slipper boots, and a fitted hoodie with some old-school holiday pattern on it. Even at the crack of dawn when I kept her up half the night making love, she still managed to look put together.

I merely slung a pair of sweats over my shoulder and followed her downstairs.

Nova spit out the paci and started waking up the entire house.

"Someone wants her presents!" I called as I walked down the hallway filled with closed doors.

Once her bottle was made and she was hungrily sucking at it, Ivy put on a pot of coffee, and everyone started appearing in the living room.

Rimmel was her usual unruly self, looking like she slept inside a tornado, and Rome looked at her like he didn't even notice.

Hell, I was beginning to think he didn't.

Drew was the last one downstairs, yawning and scratching at his unshaven jaw. He grunted, and Ivy pointed toward the kitchen where the coffee was.

Once Nova finished her bottle, she was passed around to everyone in the room for her Merry Christmas hugs and then promptly fell asleep on Drew's shoulder.

For some reason, she liked the guy.

It had to be in the genes she got from her mother.

He was just as in love with her, though, and he spent lots of hours holding her. He was a good uncle. Hell, all three of my bros were.

A mug of coffee appeared beneath my nose, and I smiled in appreciation, wrapping my hands around the cup. Ivy dropped down beside me, bouncing around all excitedly.

I chuckled and reached for her, but she pulled back.

"Hey," I intoned, looking up from the mug.

Her face was split in a huge smile, her straight white teeth all on display. In front of her she held a small green box with a huge red bow.

"Open it!" she rushed out.

"You mean there are presents for other people and not just the baby around this place?" Trent joked.

Romeo laughed.

"I told you not to get me anything," I said, even though I was charmed by her enthusiasm. I wrapped a palm around the back of her head and pulled her in. "I already have everything."

"Except for this." She held up the box and gave it a little shake. Whatever was inside rattled.

It got me curious.

I grinned and reached for it. She snatched it back. "What do you say?"

I lifted an eyebrow. She patiently waited.

"Please?" I prompted.

"B's whipped!" Romeo announced.

"Hells yeah, he is." Trent agreed.

"I'm giving you the mental equivalent to the finger right now," I told them all. "I'd do it literally, but I can't be having my daughter see such things."

"Whipped," Romeo whispered.

Rimmel giggled.

"What you laughing at, tutor girl? Can you even see around all that hair?"

She gasped and threw a pillow with a moose on it at my head.

Ivy cleared her throat impatiently, and I turned back. Even though she'd slept on her hair, it was smooth and shiny, and it just begged for my hands.

I leaned forward and kissed her softly.

She surrendered the box.

I glanced between her and it, trying to take a guess as to what it could be. "It's from all of us, not just me," she said.

Everyone was waiting, and I admit it made me curious as hell. I made short work of the bow and then tore off the green wrapping. A quick lift of the lid, and I stared down.

It was a key. One single key. Looked like an ordinary house key, one that wasn't brand new either.

I glanced up, and Ivy smiled bigger. "It unlocks something in this house."

I looked at Romeo for help. He shook his head. I turned to Rim. "Help a brother out?"

"I would, but I can't see past my hair," she cracked.

"Aww, don't be like that, sis."

Ivy tapped me on the shoulder. "There's only one locked door in this entire house."

I felt my face screw up. Snatching the key, I wandered into the kitchen, past the island, and toward the single door that opened into the garage. Everyone followed behind me. I could feel their anticipation and near giddiness.

What the hell were they up to?

I slid the key into the lock on the door and turned.

The bolt slid free.

Ivy clapped, and Romeo laughed at her. "Don't pee yourself, princess."

"I'm opening up the garage now," I announced. "If something lunges at me, I'm gonna be pissed."

The door swung open, and I reached around to turn on the overhead lights inside. They flickered to life almost instantly, and they were so bright it was almost blinding.

Or maybe it was the thing sitting inside.

Shock rendered me immobile.

I didn't speak or blink. Or breathe.

I couldn't do anything but stand there and stare at the most fucking beautiful thing I'd ever laid eyes on.

Except my wife and daughter of course.

Unable to contain herself anymore, Ivy lunged at me, wrapping her arms around my waist and squealing. "Do you like it?"

My mouth went dry.

I glanced at Romeo.

Was this for real?

He nodded.

"Fucking hell," I muttered and rubbed a hand over my face, then blinked up at the object I was sure would disappear.

It was still there.

Behind me, everyone started to snicker.

"Does that mean he doesn't like it?" Ivy worried and pulled back to look behind us.

I snagged her around the waist and pulled her back in.

"This is for me?" I asked, hoarse.

"We lied about the garage being for the owners of the house. We've been hiding this here since we got here!"

"Are you fucking for real right now!" I whooped out.

"Hells yeah." Romeo came to stand behind me, and we both admired the view.

It was a brand new truck.

But not just any truck.

A Ford F-150 Tuscany Shelby Cobra.

It was like the baddest bitch of all trucks. A souped-up Mustang in truck form. I'd never seen one in person. They were hard as hell to get ahold of. There were only twenty in Canada and not many more here in the States.

Most people had to preorder them just to get one.

And it was sitting right the fuck in front of me.

"That's mine?" I asked again, wanting to be sure.

A set of keys appeared. Romeo dangled them over my shoulder and in front of my face.

I snatched them and ran out into the garage. The cement floor was cold as ice, but I didn't care. Fuck the cold. This truck was the shit wet dreams were made of.

I looked it over almost frantically, trying to take it all in. It was bright blue with a silver-toned racing stripe that stretched across the hood, down the honeycomb grill, and all the way across the tunnel cover over the bed and down the tailgate.

It was a seven hundred horsepower, which meant it owned the freaking road.

The name Shelby was on the side, and there was a cobra logo on the front grill. It was lifted off the ground with suspension kits and boasted eighteen-inch wheels.

The interior was like the finest ass I'd ever seen. It made me want to cry. Climate controlled seats, logo embroidered headrests, and just about every bell and whistle a guy could imagine.

It was a four door, which meant it had seating for five, and I could take Nova for a ride.

Drew, Trent, and Romeo all came forward, and we went total guy mode and basically went over it with a fine-tooth comb.

It. Was. Awesome.

"So you like it?" Ivy finally said from near the garage door. Nova was in her arms, buried beneath a bunch of blankets, and Rimmel was beside her.

"I think I came in my sweats," I deadpanned. "I had a freaking orgasm right in my boxers, and I'm still sporting a hard-on for this truck."

"Eww," Rimmel drawled out.

"Sorry, sis," I said and shrugged. Some things just had to be said.

"How the hell did you guys get one of these?" Then my bubble of awe deflated. "How much did it cost?"

A little worry flashed across Ivy's face, and that made me even more anxious.

"Kiss it good-bye and let's go inside." Romeo slapped me on the back. "You can visit it later."

I felt sad when I stepped in the house away from it.

Rimmel went into the kitchen and snatched a cookie from the container and sat at the island. Romeo went over and lifted her up and sat back down with her in his lap.

"It was my idea to get you a new truck," Ivy said from close by. "Yours is older, and ever since the sugar in the gas tank thing…" Her voice faded away.

"Your truck is a piece of shit and you needed a new one," Rome deadpanned.

"My truck isn't that bad," I said, defending my ride.

"You insisted I drive the Range Rover because it was safe. Well, now I'm insisting you drive that new truck for the same reason."

"Baby, that truck cost way more than your Rover." I reasoned.

She blanched. "Are you mad?"

I made a rude sound and crossed to her. When she was in my arms, I leaned down in her ear and whispered. "I fucking love it so hard. Times two. Times ten. I could never be mad at you for doing something so awesome for me."

Truth was the price tag was probably going to give me hives. I had a kid to feed, and we were building a family compound, but what the hell? We could afford it, and now that we both had new cars and a house on the way, we wouldn't need to make any more big purchases. Besides, Anthony was working on an endorsement deal for me right now, and if I got it, then the cost of this truck would be covered.

Ivy tightened her arms around my waist for long moments, then pulled back. Her blue eyes were bright, and it reminded me of the truck. I wondered if she picked it to match her eyes.

Knowing her, she totally did.

"I told Drew I wanted to get you a new truck and asked him what kind." Ivy began.

Drew made a sound. "I opened up my latest *GearShark* magazine and pointed to an ad for it. I told her that truck was the freaking king of trucks. I never thought she'd actually try and buy one." He shook his head like he was bewildered.

Trent laughed. "She was like a damn dog with a bone."

I pinned her with a stare. "How the hell did you get ahold of the Shelby model?"

She grimaced. "I didn't. I couldn't find out anything, and the minute they saw me coming, my blond hair and slight southern accent was a neon sign for them to try and take advantage."

I felt my hackles rise. They better not have treated her like that. I'd fucking drive that truck to the lot and put it up their asses.

"That's where Romeo came in." She finished.

Ah.

Made total sense now.

Romeo always got what he wanted, and if he set his sights on that truck, then of course it was in the garage.

I turned to him, and we exchanged a look. He shrugged. "I made a call. The Ford dealership in Cali was more than happy to provide the star of the Maryland Knights with the truck of his dreams."

"So they thought it was for you?" I said.

"No. They knew exactly who it was for. I was talking about you."

Surreal.

My life was entirely surreal.

"So," I surmised and glanced at Drew and Trent. "You two picked the truck." My eyes swung to Ivy. "You chose the color and wrote the check." I looked at Romeo. "You managed to make it all happen."

"It was a total family project." Ivy agreed.

Rimmel cleared her throat. "I got you a pair of fuzzy dice to hang on the rearview mirror."

I laughed.

"I can't believe you guys did this for me." I was overcome with emotion.

"You deserve it, B," Rome said and slapped me on the back before going into the kitchen to get some more coffee.

"Thank you," I said to everyone.

"You can thank me by letting me take it for a test drive," Drew said.

"Hell no," I drawled. "No one drives that baby but me."

"We'll see about that," Trent intoned.

"Breakfast and presents!" Rimmel announced. She started bustling around the kitchen, and I pulled Ivy into the living room away from everyone.

Ivy laid the baby in her nearby sleeper and took a moment to make sure she was settled before coming back to stand before me.

"Epic. That's what you are."

"I hope you still say that after you see the bank statement." She worried.

"Nah." I scoffed. "But it sure does make what I got you look like a thrift store find."

"I don't care," she vowed. "You're everything I could ever ask for."

I cupped my hands beneath her arms and lifted, stepping back to pin her against the wall. Her legs wrapped around me, and I pressed in close.

"It matches your eyes," I murmured, still thinking of my sweet-ass truck parked just feet away.

"You noticed."

"I notice everything when it comes to you."

We started kissing and didn't come up for air until Drew stepped around the corner and started making gagging sounds.

After that, we pulled apart, and everyone piled around the tree and started handing out presents.

Like I mentioned, Nova's pile was gigantic.

It was an easy morning filled with laughter, gifts, and family.

Oh, and sprinkles. I poured that shit on my eggs.

It made them all festive-like.

The seven of us spent the entire day around a fire, with Christmas movies on TV, lights twinkling in the tree, and snow swirling just beyond the window.

We had a traditional turkey dinner that none of us cooked. It was catered, and all we had to do was heat it up and serve.

Rome and Rimmel disappeared off and on throughout the day, and I knew exactly what they were doing, because it was the same thing Ivy and I did when we managed to sneak away for stolen moments.

Even without the truck sitting in the garage, this day would have been one of the best holidays of my life.

What was even better?

It was only our first one all together. Our family had so many more ahead.

And every single one of them was going to be merry and bright.

"Merry Christmas to all,
and to all a good night."
#HappyHoliday

#BuzzBoss

#ChristmasCookies

Cookies taste better with sprinkles.

#BraedenSaysSo

#BuzzBoss

#Holiday

Recipes

Peanut Butter Blossom Cookies

Also known as "Kiss" cookies. This is a recipe straight out of my childhood. My Mommom made these every year. This is her recipe. She had a container of cookies on her counter full of Christmas cookies, and these were always a hit.

She passed this year, so this is my way of remembering her but also sharing a little piece of my memories with you. —Enjoy!

Ingredients

1 1/3 cup of flour

1 tsp. baking soda

½ tsp. salt

½ cup butter or margarine

1/3 cup peanut butter (the creamy kind)

½ cup white sugar

½ cup brown sugar

1 egg

1 tsp. vanilla

1 bag of Hershey Kiss chocolate candy

Directions

Preheat oven to 375 degrees.

Cream together butter and peanut butter. Slowly add in sugar. Next add egg and vanilla. Beat well. Slowly mix in dry ingredients.

Shape dough into very small balls. Roll each ball in sugar (you could use colored if you want or just plain white sugar).

Place balls onto a greased cookie sheet. Bake for about 8 minutes (depending on your oven). Remove from oven and press one Hershey Kiss into the center of each cookie (will flatten cookie out a bit).

Remove from cookie sheet and place on a sheet of aluminum foil to cool.

#Holiday Style Rice Krispie Treats

This is a pretty well-known recipe that I've given a twist. I make this often around the holidays because it's a little different than the traditional cookie, feeds many people, and is popular with kids. Plus, the chocolate chips add a little something extra to make it *#Holiday* special! —*Enjoy!*

Ingredients

6 cups of Rice Krispies cereal

3 Tbsp. margarine or butter

1 10 oz. package of regular marshmallows OR 4 cups of mini marshmallows

1 bag of Nestle Toll House swirled chocolate chips (sold around the holidays)

Directions

Melt butter in a large saucepan over low heat. Once melted, add in marshmallows and stir until completely melted. Remove from heat.

Add the Rice Krispies to the melted marshmallow and stir well.

Add the bag of swirled chocolate chips to the mixture and fold in (they won't melt).

Using a buttered spatula or large spoon, press the mixture into a buttered (I use cooking spray on the pan and my spatula) 13X9 pan.

Let cool, then cut into squares.

Candy Cane Cocoa

Nothing says cold, holiday weather better than a crackling fire and a warm mug filled with cocoa. This recipe takes it a step further and adds the flavor of a candy cane! —*Enjoy!*

Ingredients

4 cups of milk (Go full fat or skim. It's up to you! Just remember it will be creamier if it's not skim.)

4 candy canes crushed up (This is a good time to use the ones that always break when you pull them out of the box! You know it happens to you, too...)

3 one ounce squares of semi-sweet chocolate, chopped (your favorite kind!)

Marshmallow fluff

4 mini candy canes

Directions

In a saucepan, heat the milk over med-low heat until hot. Do not boil.

Whisk in the chopped-up chocolate and crushed candy cane pieces until everything is melted and smooth.

Divide the mixture among four mugs and garnish with a dollop of marshmallow fluff. Add a mini candy cane to each mug for a holiday effect and a stirring stick!

You can also sprinkle red sugar sprinkles over the fluff for a pretty effect.

Braeden's Brownie in a Mug

I had to get in a recipe for B! We all know how much he loves brownies and sprinkles! This is a fun, easy recipe you can make when people drop in unexpectedly during the holiday season.

Or you can just make it when you want a chocolate fix.

If you're like B, you'll probably make it every day.

Don't forget the extra sprinkles! —*Enjoy!*

Ingredients

4 Tbsp granulated sugar

4 Tbsp self-rising flour

3 Tbsp cocoa powder

1 egg

3 Tbsp milk

3 Tbsp Nutella or any hazelnut flavored spread

3 Tbsp vegetable oil

Chocolate sprinkles for topping

Chocolate icing or whipped cream for topping

Directions

Combine all ingredients into a microwave-safe mug. Whisk well - a fork works great for this!

Microwave for 1 ½ - 3 minutes. This depends on the microwave. It is suggested to check the brownie after 1 ½ minutes and then cook longer if needed.

Top brownie with a layer of chocolate icing (or whipped cream!) and a layer of chocolate sprinkles!

Traditional Chocolate Chip Cookies

You can't go wrong with a chocolate chip cookie. Warm and gooey from the oven with a glass of cold milk is pretty much a moment of magic in your mouth.

I make chocolate chip cookies every Christmas, and they always are a #HolidayHit

You can always mix it up a bit by adding colored chocolate chips, candy pieces, or nuts to this recipe to give it a special twist all your own. —Enjoy!

Ingredients

2 sticks of butter (softened, not melted)

2 eggs

¾ cup granulated sugar

¾ cup brown sugar

2 ¼ cup all-purpose flour

1 tsp. vanilla

1 tsp. baking soda

1 tsp. salt

1 bag milk chocolate or semi-sweet chocolate chips

Directions

Preheat oven to 350 degrees.

Using a mixer, beat butter and sugars together. Add eggs and vanilla, beating well. Gradually beat in all the dry ingredients until cookie dough forms and is well mixed. Stir in the bag of chocolate chips.

Drop dough by rounded tablespoons (I use a mini ice cream scoop!) onto a lined or greased baking sheet.

Bake cookies 10-13 minutes (depending on oven) until golden brown.

Remove from oven and transfer cookies to a wire rack or a sheet of foil to cool.

Good luck keeping fingers of all ages away!

No-Bake Cookies

This is a classic recipe straight out of my childhood. When I got married, my mom and Mommom (grandmother) put together a recipe book and gave it to me. My Mommom passed a couple years ago, and I always feel so nostalgic around the holidays because I always spent them with her. It's special to be able to pull out the book and see the recipes written by her hand. This is one of those recipes. —*Enjoy!*

Ingredients

2 cups sugar

¼ cup cocoa

½ cup milk

½ cup margarine (1 stick)

½ cup peanut butter (creamy)

3 cups oatmeal

¼ tsp. salt

1 tsp. vanilla

Directions

In a pot, mix sugar, cocoa, milk, and margarine.

Cook over medium heat until mixture comes to a boil.

Remove from heat and add peanut butter, salt, and vanilla.

Stir until blended.

Add oatmeal.

Drop by teaspoons onto waxed paper and let cool.

Snickerdoodles

This is another special recipe given to me by Mommom. There is something especially sweet about a snickerdoodle cookie. Maybe it's the simplicity of them. Or maybe it's the sugar! —*Enjoy!*

Ingredients

½ cup butter (1 stick)

½ cup shortening

1 ½ cups sugar

2 eggs

1 tsp. vanilla

2 ¾ cups flour

2 tsp. cream of tartar

1 tsp. baking soda

¼ tsp. salt

Cinnamon and sugar mixture to roll cookies in

Directions

Preheat oven to 375 degrees.

Mix together all the wet ingredients, then add in all the dry.

Shape dough into small balls.

Roll each ball in mixture of cinnamon and sugar.

Place each ball 2 inches apart on a cookie sheet.

Bake the cookies at 375 for 8-10 minutes or until just slightly brown.

Remove cookies from oven and transfer to aluminum foil to cool.

White Hot Chocolate

This is a rich, sinful cup of goodness. Perfect for a cold day with a book, a movie, or even in front of the tree on Christmas morning! —*Enjoy!*

Ingredients

2 cups heavy cream

6 cups whole milk

12 ounces finely chopped white chocolate

1 tsp. vanilla

1 block dark chocolate

Directions

Using a potato peeler, shave the dark chocolate into curls and set aside for later.

Place the white chocolate in a medium heat-proof bowl.

Pour milk and cream into a medium saucepan and place over medium heat until bubbles begin to form around the edges (takes approximately 4 minutes).

Do NOT boil. (Boiling will result in something you *don't* want to drink on Christmas. Or ever.)

Remove the pan from the heat and immediately pour over the white chocolate.

As the chocolate begins to melt, stir to combine.

Whisk in vanilla and continue whisking until a light foam forms.

Serve in mugs, add whipped cream or marshmallows, and sprinkle with the dark chocolate curls for garnish!

Cheese Ball

Looking for something that isn't sweet? Something that you can take to a party or set out to nibble on while you wrap a mountain of gifts? Look no further! Cheese Ball is here.

This recipe is from my handy recipe book, the one my Mom and Mommom put together. Looking at it today, I remembered that my best friend's mom also added in recipes for me! So this one is hers. Thanks, Jane!

—Enjoy!

Ingredients

2 eight-ounce blocks of cream cheese

¼ cup chopped green peppers

1 small can crushed pineapple (drained)

2 tbsp. onion flakes

1 tbsp. seasoned salt

Crushed pecans for rolling

Directions

Mix all ingredients well.

Shape the mixture into two balls (or two logs) and roll them in crushed pecans.

Place cheese ball on a platter and serve with bread, crackers, pretzels… anything you want!

Gluten-Free Pumpkin Bread

This is a favorite of mine. I am pretty much obsessed with pumpkin, and I make this in my house all the time, not just for the holidays. However, pumpkin is decidedly one of the most popular flavors of the season. Since I am gluten free, I had to find a way to enjoy my pumpkin obsession (outside of a latte, of course) in a way that didn't make my body unhappy! If anyone in your life is gluten free, this will be a real treat!

—*Enjoy!*

Ingredients

3 eggs

1 cup regular sugar and a ¼ cup brown sugar

1 tsp. vanilla

1 cup pumpkin puree (*not* pumpkin pie filling)

1/3 cup oil

1 ½ cups all-purpose gluten-free flour (I think Bob's Red Mill is the best, but you can use any. Or traditional flour if you don't need it to be gluten free.)

1 tsp. baking soda

½ tsp. baking powder

1 tbsp. cinnamon (I use a lot. Cut this in half if desired.)

½ tsp. ginger

1 tsp. salt

½ tsp. pumpkin pie spice

Directions

Preheat oven to 350 degrees.

Combine all wet ingredients and mix with an electric mixer.

Add in dry ingredients gradually, until everything is combined.

Pour into a greased bread pan and bake for 50-55 minutes (until a knife inserted into the center comes out clean).

Cool (if you can wait that long), cut, and eat!

Peanut Butter Fudge

Another recipe out of my recipe book! It's easy and sure to please a crowd! —Enjoy!

Ingredients

3 cups sugar

1 tsp. vanilla

6 tbsp. cocoa

¾ cup milk (regular or 2%)

7 ½ ounces marshmallow crème

12 ounces peanut butter

Directions

In a bowl, combine the marshmallow crème and peanut butter. Set aside.

In a medium saucepan, combine sugar, vanilla, cocoa, and milk.

Boil for three minutes (*only* three minutes!).

Immediately pour over the crème and peanut butter mixture.

Mix well.

Pour into a greased 9 x 13 glass dish and allow to harden.

Best Ever Apple Pie

This is my recipe for apple pie. I truly think it's the best apple pie. I featured this recipe in the back of my novel *Text*. I make it around the holidays, and it's always a treat. You can serve it with ice cream, whipped cream, or, as some enjoy, in a bowl with milk! —*Enjoy!*

Ingredients

You can use store-bought crust or make your own.

To make a double pie crust:

2 2/3 cups all-purpose flour

1 tsp. salt

½ cup butter and a ½ cup shortening

6 tbsp. ice-cold water

Apple Pie Filling:

4-8 Granny Smith apples (depends on size)

4 tbsp. cut-up butter and a ½ cup granulated sugar

2 tbsp. ground cinnamon (I like a lot of cinnamon. You can cut this in half.)

1 tbsp. all-purpose flour (This helps the sauce thicken.)

Directions

Preheat oven to 400 degrees.

To make crust:

Cut together the flour, salt, butter, and shortening with a pastry fork until blended.

Add water one tablespoon at a time and mix with fork until it firms into a ball.

Separate the ball into two smaller balls.

Roll each out onto a heavily floured surface, flipping over frequently.

Place one crust in the bottom of a pie pan and reserve the other crust for topping the pie.

To make filling:

Peel and slice all the apples. Add all slices into a bowl.

Mix the apples with the sugar, cinnamon, and flour until well coated.

Dump apple mixture into pie crust.

Place the 4 tablespoons of cut-up butter randomly on top of the apples.

Cover the pie with the remaining crust and crimp the edges together.

With a sharp knife, cut a few slits in the top crust (to allow steam to escape while baking), and then you can brush the top of the pie with an egg wash (egg wash = a beaten raw egg). This will give the crust its golden-brown appearance.

Sprinkle granulated sugar over the top of the crust, which will give the pie a nice flavor and sweetness.

Bake for 40-50 minutes, depending on oven.

Overnight Pumpkin French Toast Bake

This is another family favorite. It's perfect for Christmas morning, or any morning really! It's really great because you make it the night before. Then all you have to do is pull it out, pop it in the oven, and enjoy some coffee while it bakes! I love it so much I featured this recipe in the back of my novel *Tattoo*. Go ahead and give it a try! —*Enjoy!*

Ingredients

1 loaf of French bread (Or any type of bread you have. It's roughly 5-7 cups of bread, cubed.)

7 eggs

½ cup pumpkin puree

2 cups milk (I use almond milk. You can use what you prefer.)

1 tsp. vanilla extract

1 ½ tsp. ground cinnamon

Shake of ginger (I literally shake the spice canister over the bowl to add a little.)

Shake of nutmeg

3-4 tbsp. brown sugar for topping

Directions

Tear or cut the bread into chunks or bite-size pieces.

Place bread cubes into a lightly greased 9 x 13 baking dish and set aside.

In a mixing bowl, combine the seven eggs, pumpkin, milk, vanilla, and spices.

Pour the egg mixture over the bread cubes. Then press down lightly on the bread to soak the mixture through.

Once the bread is moist, cover the dish tightly with a lid or plastic wrap.

Refrigerate overnight.

In the morning (Good morning!), preheat your oven to 350 degrees.

Sprinkle the brown sugar over top of the French toast (Be as generous as you like).

Bake the French toast for 35-45 minutes.

Serve warm with syrup or honey drizzled over the top (I also put butter on mine!).

Rum Cake

This recipe is from Adrienne Ambrose, the special lady who runs the *#Hashtag* Pinterest board. I think it makes a great addition to the holiday table. Especially if you love some rum! Adrienne also let me know that this recipe is an old one, so in addition to alcohol, it's soaked in tradition! —*Enjoy!*

Ingredients

For cake

1 box Pillsbury yellow cake mix with pudding

2 tbsp. orange peel

Jamaican Rum

For Coating

1 stick of butter, melted

¾ cup sugar

¼ cup water

Directions

Bake cake according to box directions, substituting water for Jamaican Rum and adding the orange peel to the batter.

Use bundt cake or Turks head pan if available.

To make the coating:

In a saucepan, cook butter, sugar, and water over medium heat, stirring well and often until all the ingredients are smooth.

Bring to a boil, then simmer for two minutes.

Remove from heat and add one cup of Jamaican rum, stir, and taste. If you want a stronger flavor (or to knock out Uncle Bob), add more rum.

Using a pastry brush, brush over cake, letting it drip down the sides, while cake is hot.

Give each sweep a chance to be absorbed into the cake before applying next sweep. This step will take multiple sweeps to fully absorb into cake.

Cake will be shiny and moist on the outside.

For added garnish and flavor, you can top with halved walnuts.

Cover with plastic wrap and store in refrigerator.

Potato Chip Cookies

This recipe is also courtesy of Adrienne Ambrose, the special lady who runs the *#Hashtag* Pinterest board! She told me this is her Nana's recipe. Sounds pretty interesting, right? I mean, potato chips AND cookies? I don't know why, but something about this one screams Drew and Trent. I can just imagine them inhaling these!

—*Enjoy!*

Ingredients

1 cup butter or margarine

½ cup sugar

1 egg yolk

1 tsp. vanilla

1 ½ cups all-purpose flour

½ cup crushed potato chips

½ cup chopped nuts (optional)

Powder sugar to coat cookies

Directions

Cream butter and sugar, then add remaining ingredients.

Drop by teaspoonful onto ungreased cookie sheet.

Bake at 350 degrees for 15 minutes.

Cool slightly, then roll in powdered sugar.

Rimmel's Healthy Dog Treats

You know Rimmel would never leave her pets out of the holiday fun. Any dog lover will agree that pets love goodies, too! Here is an easy and fun way to include them in the holiday season. —*Enjoy!*

Ingredients

4 ½ cups oatmeal (any kind you prefer)

1 medium apple

1 egg

1 cup pumpkin puree

Directions

Preheat oven to 400 degrees.

Put oatmeal into a blender or food processor and chop until fine.

Grate the apple and add to oatmeal (Be careful not to get any of the seeds and core in the mixture).

Add pumpkin and egg to bowl. Mix all together. Mixture will be thick.

Roll the dough out on a floured surface (You can use some of the ground oatmeal!) until it is approximately a half-inch thick.

Use cookie cutters in any shape you like (Rimmel likes small candy canes!).

Bake the cookies approximately twelve minutes or until crispy.

Cool and keep in an airtight container for up to one week.

Crepes

This is a traditional recipe passed down through my husband's family, who is French-Canadian. They have crepes for almost every occasion. You can fill them with something savory or sweet, your choice!

—*Enjoy!*

Ingredients

4 eggs

1 1/3 cups milk

2 tbsp. melted butter

1 cup flour

½ tsp. salt

1 tsp. vanilla

Directions

Mix all ingredients in a bowl.

In my family, we let the batter sit overnight in the fridge, but if you're too hungry to wait, you can cook immediately.

In a skillet or round, flat pan, melt butter or spray with non-stick spray.

Add a small ladle of the batter in the center of the pan and gently tilt pan around until the batter covers the bottom in a thin layer.

Let cook over medium/low heat (It won't take long because they are super thin!).

Flip over and cook for an additional minute.

Move to a platter or plate.

You can fill these with any kind of ingredient you like. Fruit, whipped cream, etc. My family enjoys them with butter and brown sugar, rolled, and drizzled with syrup.

Eggnog Mudslide

I have to admit… I'm not an eggnog fan. But so many of you are, including members of my own family! So I had to include something eggnog in this holiday recipe extravaganza! And I have to say I might not like eggnog much, but this recipe looks amazing! I have a feeling it would make Romeo say, "Hells Yeah!" —*Enjoy!*

Ingredients

Kahlúa

Vodka (your favorite brand)

Eggnog (any brand)

Whipped cream

Nutmeg for garnish

Cinnamon sticks for garnish

Directions

In a cocktail shaker or tall glass, combine one part Kahlúa, one part vodka, and two parts eggnog.

Shake or stir well and strain into glasses (or *one* glass if that darned Uncle Bob is over).

Add whipped cream and sprinkle with nutmeg.

Add cinnamon stick if desired!

*This beverage is intended for adults over the age of twenty-one. Please remember to drink responsibly.

**This recipe was found on Pinterest.

Peanut Butter Temptations

I make these little cookies every year for my family and friends. I've given them to teachers, too. They're probably my most popular cookie every year. They are always the first to be eaten in my house. They're easy, too! —Enjoy!

Ingredients

One bag of peanut butter cup minis, unwrapped

½ cup butter (1 stick)

½ cup sugar

½ cup brown sugar

½ cup creamy peanut butter (any brand)

1 egg

½ teaspoon vanilla extract

1 ½ cups all-purpose flour

¾ tsp. baking soda

½ tsp. salt

One or two mini muffin tins

Directions

Line or spray mini muffin tins.

Preheat oven to 375 degrees.

With an electric mixer, beat butter, sugars, eggs, peanut butter, and vanilla until fluffy.

Gradually beat in all dry ingredients.

Shape the dough into small, round balls and place one in each muffin cup. *Do not flatten the ball.*

Bake for approximately ten minutes. Cookies will be puffed up and lightly brown.

Remove from oven.

Press one peanut butter cup into each cookie (still in the muffin tins).

Allow to cool, then remove from muffin tins.

Eggnog French Toast

This recipe comes courtesy of one of my writing besties. Amber Garza is a young adult author with lots of titles under her belt. You should check her out sometime if you haven't already. When I told her about my project, I knew I wanted to include one of her recipes, and this is the one she gave me! About the recipe, Amber says, "I make it for Christmas morning because it's easy and I can prep the night before!"

—Enjoy!

Ingredients

8 large eggs

2 cups eggnog

Cinnamon to taste

1 loaf Texas toast

Directions

Cut the bread in half, into triangles, and lay flat in glass baking dish.

Mix together eggs, eggnog, and cinnamon and pour over the top of the bread.

Cover and refrigerate overnight.

In the morning, take bread slices and place them on a buttered cookie sheet.

Bake at 450 degrees for 10 minutes.

Sprinkle with powdered sugar.

Serve with butter and syrup!

Monkey Bread Muffins

Another perfect recipe for Christmas morning! These are easy, comforting, and so good. They also appear in the back of my romantic suspense novel *Amnesty*. I made them for my family (to taste test the recipe for you guys!), and they loved them. They were gone in two days! —*Enjoy!*

Ingredients

3 cans of cinnamon rolls (any brand)

1 can apple pie filling

½ cup raisins (optional)

¼ cup brown sugar

¼ cup granulated sugar

1 tbsp. flour

1 tsp. cinnamon

1 tsp. salt

2 tbsp. melted butter

4 tbsp. milk (any kind)

Foil muffin liners

Directions

Preheat oven to 350 degrees.

Place apple pie filling into a bowl, cut into small pieces.

To the apples, add in brown sugar, granulated sugar, flour, half of the cinnamon (reserving the other half for the glaze), and the melted butter.

Remove biscuits from cans and cut into small pieces.

Combine and mix the biscuit pieces into the apple mixture.

Spoon into muffin tins lined with foil cups. Fill each cup about three-fourths full.

Bake for about 25 minutes, depending on oven.

Glaze

While muffins are baking, combine milk, powdered sugar, and cinnamon in a bowl.

Drizzle over muffins when they come out of the oven.

If you prefer, you can use the premade icing that comes with the cinnamon rolls.

AUTHOR'S NOTE

Just know I'm grateful for you.

I want to wish you all the very best in the New Year. I hope you achieve everything you set out to do and more. And if you don't? That's okay, too.

I don't usually make resolutions because, let's be real, I never keep them. LOL. Why bother? All I know is I plan to keep writing, and I hope you keep reading. I hope I can create a few books that are even half as well received as the *Hashtag Series*.

Enjoy the season. Enjoy each other. Be safe and be happy.

I'll see you next year.

XOXO,

Cambria

Cambria Hebert is an award winning, bestselling novelist of more than twenty books. She went to college for a bachelor's degree, couldn't pick a major, and ended up with a degree in cosmetology. So rest assured her characters will always have good hair.

Besides writing, Cambria loves a caramel latte, staying up late, sleeping in, and watching movies. She considers math human torture and has an irrational fear of chickens (yes, chickens). You can often find her running on the treadmill (she'd rather be eating a donut), painting her toenails (because she bites her fingernails), or walking her chorkie (the real boss of the house).

Cambria has written within the young adult and new adult genres, penning many paranormal and contemporary titles. Her favorite genre to read and write is romantic suspense. A few of her most recognized titles are: *The Hashtag Series, Text, Torch,* and *Tattoo.*

Cambria Hebert owns and operates Cambria Hebert Books, LLC.

You can find out more about Cambria and her titles by visiting her website: http://www.cambriahebert.com.